G

The Ghastling

NO CHILDREN'S TICKETS SOLD ....IT'S TOO SPOOKY!

are you BRAVE ?

OF 'CORPSE' IT'S ALL IN FUN— BUT TO PLAY SAFE AMBULANCES & NURSES ON CALL AT ALL TIMES !

PLUS HORROR MOVIE! GIRLS! Bring Your Boy Friend ! LEARN If He's MAN Or MOUSE!

THE FETCH would like to thank Patreon supporter, AARON SPINK, for sponsoring his omen and keeping impending death alive ...

THE FETCH
ILLUSTRATION BY ANDREW ROBINSON

EDITOR
Rebecca Parfitt

ASSISTANT EDITOR
Rhys Owain Williams

GRAPHIC DESIGNER
Wallace McBride

SOCIAL MEDIA MANAGER
April-Jane Rowan

SPECIAL THANKS

J&C Parfitt, Andrew Robinson, Zuzanna Kwiecien & Claire L. Smith

CONTACT THE GHASTLING

EDITOR@THEGHASTLING.COM
WWW.THEGHASTLING.COM
SOCIAL MEDIA: @THEGHASTLING

ISSN: 2514-815X
ISBN: 978-1-8381891-2-9

PUBLISHED BY THE GHASTLING

The Ghastling gratefully acknowledges the financial support of the Books Council of Wales.

YES NO

ABCDEFGHIJKLM
NOPQRSTUVWXYZ
1234567890

~ GOOD BYE ~

THE GHASTLING

EDITORIAL

REBECCA PARFITT

ILLUSTRATION BY ANDREW ROBINSON

I am calling this issue, 'the Inhabitants issue' as this was a startlingly consistent recurring theme throughout this submissions window. Perhaps because we've all been home much more; we've all been much more observant of our domestic surroundings; much more aware of the habits of our neighbours and our housemates, partners and family; the uninvited and the other has made itself known ... Perhaps you've only just noticed there's something very, very wrong with your neighbourhood. And what about your children? Are they behaving as they should? Or has the word 'feral' crossed your mind a few times lately? Well, we have an array of stories of strange neighbours, otherness, weird tenants, uninvited inhabitants, cabin fever, possessed workmates and haunted children so you can be at ease knowing that you are not alone... And to keep you amused during the darkest part of the year, we have included amongst these pages a 'cut-out-and-keep' Ouija board* in case you wish to make friends with that knocking sound in your airing cupboard.

In *The Shadow Book of Ji Yun*[1] – *Chinese Imperial Librarian and Investigator of the Strange* (a fascinating book of recently revived and collected fragments of true encounters and accounts with the supernatural and the strange, from his findings as chief editor of the *Siku Quanshu* imperial library project, 1771.) He states in his chapter, 'A Note on Conjured Spirits':

'HUMAN BEINGS are the instruments for communication (with the spirit world) in ways far more significant than simply lending a hand or a voice (…) The spirits' communication is profoundly filtered and affected by the peculiarities of our personalities: our intelligence, our sense of humour, our senses – just as a container affects the taste of wine or individual incarnations express the soul differently in each cycle of reincarnation.'

SO, IT SEEMS, it really is down to us when it comes to 'what we invite in' and what follows. Our essence of being plays a vital role in what will haunt us. And this, my friends, is demonstrated superbly with the stories at hand:

Timothy Granville's terrifying tale, 'The Children' resonates with that of the true accounts of the Enfield hauntings and the Battersea poltergeist – an exhausted mother notices strange and disturbing goings on surrounding her children; something their father does not wish to acknowledge, at first. In 'Stick' by Matthew G. Rees, a tenant of a dilapidated old cottage cannot pay his rent. Eviction is on the cards. One day, on a usual stroll along the beach, he finds a walking stick, then a pair of glasses and then he doesn't seem quite so alone as before … In Janice Leadingham's superb ghost story of pearls and cats, 'The Keeping of Pearls', a lady buys a house, but soon after moving in it seems clear that the previous owner has not yet fully moved out, or on … a psychic convinces her the only way

---

[1] ed. trans. Yu, Yi Izzy & Yu Branscum, John, The Shadow Book of Ji Yun – Imperial Librarian and Investigator of the Strange, Empress Wu Books, 2021, p.88.

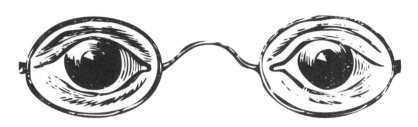

to solve the problem is by getting a cat. Verity Holloway's 'The Fireman', a ghost story set in the late 19th century aboard a ship, The Anvil, travelling through Portugal whose inhabitants are plagued with misfortune: accidents and strange visions. The ship's doctor is overwhelmed. One patient reports seeing a man inside the furnace and the story unfolds with a delicious creepiness and mounting anxiety – not a good combination when aboard a ship ... 'Oasis' by Anna Ojinnaka is a story set in the harsh and beautiful terrain of the desert. The lives of a married couple are shaken when one day she disappears only to reappear nine days later apparently unscathed – almost revitalised – by her experience but it soon becomes clear that something is very different about her, not least her appetite for meat and sex ... Ashley Stokes' brilliantly mind-bending story and future-folk horror 'Black Slab' is a distorted tale – electric with paranoia – of a couple existing in a post apocalyptic bubble of madness, which is exacerbated by the arrival of a large black wardrobe. Well, we've all done it haven't we? We've all ordered something we don't need in a fit of desperation, right? In Mike Adamson's eery timeslip tale 'The Heaviest Burden' a thief-to-order is commissioned to steal a WWII document belonging to Hitler from an aviation museum, but as he gets closer to the task in hand things get really creepy and he is reminded of what once inhabited these museum artefacts ... Simon John Parkin's tale, 'The Ran-tan Man' tells of some squatters moving into an empty house, wreaking havoc with the neighbours. Something needs to be done about them so someone suggests they make a Ran-tan Man and try to oust them. But things take a very sinister turn in this Wickerman-esque folk-horror. Sinéad Persaud's horror story, 'Thread', set against the backdrop of Victorian London and the Whitechapel murders, tells the tale of a dressmaker's apprentice and her unfortunate and very unusual demise. Note: if you think a mannequin's eyes are following you, they probably are ...

We hope you enjoy this issue as much as we have in putting it together. However you intend to spend your winter hours, us and the inhabitants will keep you company. Thanks as always go to you, our reader, and to the patrons that keep Ghastling Towers at ghost-happy temperature.

See you in the spring!

Rebecca Parfitt

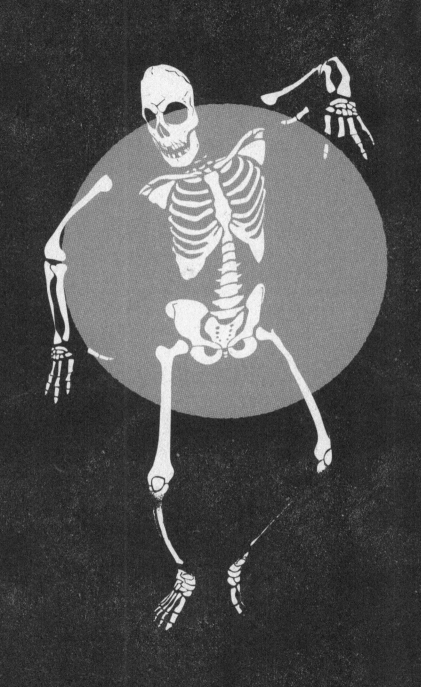

THE CHILDREN

by Timothy Granville

*F*rom *the moment* it starts, Lilian knows it's the children. The children must be doing it. The only question is whether or not they're working together. Sally, of course, can't really be involved.

She's too young, too clumsy, even if the others convinced her to take part she would give it all away. Blab about what they did in the night while Mummy and Daddy were sleeping. Forget to wash the grime off her hands and confess through snot and tears. No, neither of them would be fool enough to trust Sally. So is it Anne, or Charles, or both?

At first, she suspects Anne. She's the bossy one, the eldest, and my goodness a difficult age. And it starts with that awful record player she convinced them to buy. They'd had words about the racket already, Lilian seemed to spend half her life shouting up the stairs. But then Anne began to complain that it was broken. The thing was sticking, playing a screaming noise over and over, one of her pop singers screaming. 'How do you tell the difference?' Guy asked, smiling, unlit king-size wagging in his mouth. But he went up to her room and came down again without his smile. And then it kept happening, in the middle of the night. The two of them blundering half-asleep through Anne's door – 'What on earth is going on in here, young lady?' And Anne looking around as though she's still groggy and confused and just starting to panic – if it's a performance, it's a beautiful one, really – saying in a little-girl voice, 'It wasn't me, Daddy. Mummy? It wasn't me.'

Soon they are woken by noises practically every night. They go downstairs to find the house is a shambles. The books have been swept from their shelves, the new rug is strewn with soil from the smashed pot plants, the rubbish has been emptied across the floor. There are nameless stains smeared on the walls, sometimes Lilian discovers gobbets of dung or offal. God knows where they get them from.

For the umpteenth time, she and Guy assemble the puffy-eyed children in front of the mess. They try everything: threats, punishments, wheedling, even begging – she begs them, that is, while Guy looks away. They make them clean up, but they are so sloppy that Lilian has to do it all over again once they've finished. And they remain adamant. It wasn't them, it's never them. Sometimes Anne says to ask Charles about it, and sometimes Charles says they should ask Anne. Sally only stares.

Though she sleeps poorly at the best of times, Lilian decides she has to stay awake all night. She must catch them at it, there's no other way. So she lies fully dressed on the bed, hour after hour, listening to Guy's breathing. When her eyelids sag, she pinches herself, claws at her thickening midriff. Guy starts snoring, she heaves a sigh. But then she realises it isn't him. Downstairs there is a low guttural noise, a weird grunting.

She is quite awake now in the dark, as frightened as she can ever remember being.

'Guy?'

'What?...What's time?'

'Guy, Guy, there's an animal. Something.'

He sits up in bed. 'Christ.'

The noise is moving all over the house. 'The children,' she says.

Guy reaches for the old baluster he keeps under the bed – they are alone out here, no neighbours in earshot. He is snapping on the light, throwing open the door, club in hand, ready to defend his family. But that isn't what she meant.

Of course, they find the children apparently asleep, and, of course, by the time they've rounded them up the grunting has stopped. Guy goes downstairs and sees nothing out of place. As they're making their way back to bed, Charles says, 'What's that pong?' And it's true, the house smells ungodly, like rancid meat, but they say never mind, never mind, it's not that bad, only the drains. They dispatch the children, then lie beside each other for the rest of the night, staring at the slowly-lightening ceiling.

When they come down the next morning, the stench is gone but there are obscenities written on the walls in dark sludge. This is too much for Guy, who bawls out the children, threatening to take his belt to them. Though they cry, that's all. No confessions, no telling tales. Poor Guy hasn't a chance.

Lilian wanders from room to room in an under-slept stupor. Part of her just wants to cry too at the day of scrubbing ahead, but another part of her is trying to work out how they've managed it. She has barely dozed since those disgusting animal noises. It's hard to imagine one of them creeping down and doing all this and sneaking back upstairs during her brief early-morning dreams. In the hallway the scrawl is enough to make her blush. Where could Anne have learnt such words, or to think of herself that way? But Charles has always been sly, perhaps he's used them to frame her. She remembers once when he was quite small she caught him writing Anne's name on the stairs with a crayon. Yes, it could be Charles. But then where has he learnt them?

The next week is appalling. Lilian finds strange deposits of muck in places that they can't be – drawers she opened a minute ago, rooms she's only just left. One morning, she glimpses a dinner plate sailing down the kitchen, shattering against the far end. A cabinet topples of its own accord, Guy's sporting trophies fling themselves from the mantelpiece. She notices too that some of the stains covering the house appear to be seeping *out* from the walls. On Sunday, as they sit down to lunch, all five of them get a simultaneous nosebleed. Lilian stares at her family over her cupped hands, bewilderment – or what looks like it – on every face. The blood spatters the napkins, her best tablecloth, the steaming joint.

Later, once the children are in bed and Guy is on his third scotch of the night, she decides to say it.

'It's them, you know.'

He rubs his eyes. 'So we've agreed.'

'Today, at the table. That was them.'

The tumbler slams on the sideboard. 'What the hell are you talking about, woman?'

She looks at him, steadily, for a long time. 'You know exactly what I mean.'

They say no more about it. When Guy comes home from work the following evening, he announces that the firm have asked him to meet with a big client in the Midlands. He'll be gone a few days. It's a last minute job, Campbell has come down with a bug. He's sorry, but it can't be helped. Lilian asks whether he'll be taking Miss Petersen this time. He searches for something in his briefcase, says he doesn't

think that will be necessary.

Lilian lies awake all night. Around three, the noises begin. She wakes Guy up to hear what he's leaving her with. At first a greedy snuffle, then the rumbling grunts in room after room, rooting through the house. Guy is flippant, but obviously afraid. She wonders if he's really worth trying to hold on to after all.

He goes first thing, grinding the Daimler's gears in his hurry to get away. So it is her and the children. She listens to them moving stealthily around the house, without their usual uproar. They are circling, biding their time. Later that morning, she discovers Sally hidden under the kitchen table with a photo album and a pair of compasses she must have taken from Anne's desk, methodically mutilating the family pictures. She is suddenly unsure about Sally. Despite everything, this comes as a shock.

Now it starts in earnest. The children complain of voices behind the walls in the night, taking turns to stop her sleeping, opening the bedroom door shivering and wide-eyed. The rooms fill up with silent, invisible clouds of flies. She feels them drumming on her face, invading her nostrils and ears and mouth. The children make a great fuss about it, but naturally she can't show them much sympathy. Charles is pelted by lumps of coal erupting from the scuttle. She wipes the black dust off his face and dabs TCP on the grazes and shampoos the living-room carpet. The bathtub and sinks fill with mire. She fishes out the clots and scours the porcelain white. She washes the floors and repaints the blemished walls and cleans and cleans until her hands are chapped and her eyes sting with chemicals. She will not let the house be ruined too.

Most of the time, the children avoid her. When she is downstairs, they keep to the upper floors, and vice versa. Now and then she catches them whispering together behind a half-closed door, but in general she is too busy to prevent it.

'Don't think I don't know,' she tells them at mealtimes. 'Just wait till your father gets home.'

The looks Anne gives her, she's barely recognisable as her daughter. And the others say they're sorry, but it doesn't stop. And if they were really sorry, they wouldn't have begun it all in the first place.

There comes a lull, at last. For twenty-four hours, the house is untroubled. Lilian eyes the children over the rim of her teacup, wondering what has changed. Charles and Sally squabble over the usual petty things, Anne gets exasperated with Charles and orders Sally around like normal. The nightmare has been left behind like something they've tired of, a toy abandoned in the middle of another room. Could it be they've grown out of it? Or is this just a ploy?

Either way, she's grateful for the rest. She sends the children upstairs early that evening and has a long bath. Afterwards, she helps herself to one of Guy's whiskies and lies on the sofa, a paperback tented on her chest. She is glad of her house's high ceilings, the freshly-painted walls. She goes to bed tired and clean.

In the night, she wakes from a dream. Something about soothing babies, she can't entirely remember. She lies there in the middle of the bed, warm and muzzy, undecided between trying to piece it together and surrendering to sleep again. Then she hears the thumping beneath her.

The lights are bright on the landing. Sally's door is ajar, there is a light in here too. The room looks as though it's been ransacked, smells like a sty. The little bed is wet through and covered in blood and vomit. There is no Sally, only a couple of damp half-footprints leading outside. Lilian follows them towards the noises, feeling curiously detached, everything very slow and clear. She spots where a child has brushed against the staircase wall, leaving a faint, bloody spoor. She makes a note of it for later.

Beneath her footfalls, she becomes aware of another sound. A kind of diffuse hiss, vast like the sea: she thinks of breakers sucked back over shingle. But there's no time to work out where it's coming from.

The children are in the living room, at the far end by the patio doors. They look like they're trying to escape from something. Lilian's bunch of house keys lies discarded on the parquet and now Anne is attempting to swing a standard lamp at the doors. She seems weak, the stem twists free of her grip, the base raises a deadened note from the glass without quite threatening to break it. Charles and Sally gasp on their hands and knees, struggling for breath. All three of them are filthy, their pyjamas soiled. Their faces are red masks, stained with the blood still running from their noses.

One after the other they catch sight of Lilian where she stands in the living room doorway. They look terrified. Anne tries to say something, but Lilian can't make it out. What's happened, why can't they talk to her? What's wrong with them?

As she watches the children, she registers that sound of the sea again. No, not the sea, she's hearing a voice. It's soft, but all around her. It is saying, *'Shh...Shh...'*

After another moment, she realises that it's her voice. She's the one saying it.

She puts a hand over her mouth. The children sink to the floor, drawing rasping breath. They start to cry.

The sense of unreality is lifting. Lilian sees the house in disarray, her husband gone, the children dirty and snivelling. A sick feeling wells in the pit of her stomach. She walks forwards, saying, 'It's all right, it's all right. You'll be fine. Come now, be brave.'

Sally screams. Anne puts her arms round her, glaring. 'Why?'

Lilian shakes her head. 'Dear, I don't know what you mean.'

'Why do you hate us?'

'I...I don't...What sort of...?'

'Stop it, mother! Just stop it!'

Lilian keeps on shaking her head. Eventually, she says, 'You need some time to calm down. I'll run the bath.'

She turns away. Leaving the living room, she notices her thriller still lying on the sofa. It is like seeing something from another lifetime, a dress she once wore to a dance.

Lilian walks on through the silent house. She tries to think about practical matters, getting the children washed and stowed safely in bed, starting on the worst of the mess. But she keeps going back to what just happened. Anne clutching Sally like that, as though protecting her from her own mother. And what on earth did she mean, hate them? They are her life. She has given them everything. Why would she say it?

She finds herself staring into the churning bathwater, with no clear memory of coming upstairs. She watches the level rise. By the time the bath is nearly full, she begins to see. She turns off the taps, smiling quickly at Guy's shaving mirror as she catches her misted reflection. Isn't that so often the way?

Her very first thought was right. It has been Anne all along.

STICK

by Matthew G. Rees

Crab Cottage – Sunday Night

Voyle has been here.

Just now.

At my door.

He didn't announce himself vocally. There was no need. I knew him from his knock (and, before that, his step-cum-stomp on the path, his surly shove of the garden gate).

Knock is putting it mildly. It was the angry, violent clatter of a clenched fist. The door fair shook in its jamb.

He must have seen the lights – faint as they are – from my candles and fire. That's why he came: storming here... over the fields... with 'drink' in him, I don't doubt.

Naturally, I didn't answer. Not at this time of night. God knows what the man is capable of. He's a brute, all right.

'Time's running out! You hear me?' he bellowed.

I seemed to smell his sickly fumes... to feel the spatter of his spittle, as if it were on my face.

He cursed, and – like a great, black cloud – lumbered away.

Stopping, for a moment, he fired a final volley.

'I won't wait forever. A week!

That's all you've got!'

Rising from my desk, I went and stood to one side of the parlour window (where I felt I wouldn't be seen).

Over the hedge, I saw his horrible hulk... making off: bristling, malevolent, darker than the night at his shoulder.

Monday

Attempting to forget the night's disturbance, I went down to, and wandered, the beach.

On the shore, I discovered a stick.

By which I mean a proper, thumb-cleft, walking stick.

So strange to see it lying there: an 'instrument'... purposeful and precise – amid the wet, black weed and the driftwood of a more ragged kind.

The waves washed it to my feet.

I picked it up.

Walking back to the cottage with it, I had the curious sense that it knew the way.

It seemed to swing, anticipating my stride, my thumb snug at home in its 'V'.

On my return, a less welcome find: another letter from Williams – Voyle's solicitor in the town.

In it, the same threats as made by his master, albeit more formally couched: fail to settle my rent arrears within seven days, and I shall be evicted.

Its author tabulated the amount.

The sum is a scandal, given the state of this place: no electricity, turbid water that I must winch from a well, walls wringing with damp, floorboards that are rotten, a 'garden' gone utterly wild.

I should, of course, be packing my bags... of my own volition... suing *them*. But what's at stake is the roof over my head. And – for now – Crab Cottage is the only one I have.

Tuesday

Although keeping his distance (after a fashion), my landlord has – in his oafish way – been spying on me.

I saw him this morning in the lane. He pretended to be transporting some sheep (which were on the back of his pickup). However, 'observing' me, I don't doubt, was his real intent.

I came upon him while walking back from the village, with some groceries from the shop.

He'd parked in the gateway of a field with a view of the cottage on its cliff edge above the sea.

My sudden appearance flustered him. But he soon regained his familiar scorn.

'Been shopping, I see,' he said, putting down a window in his vehicle.

I thought how ugly he was, and quietly cursed my life for leaving me at the mercy of such a fiend.

'Well,' he went on, 'if you can afford to spend money on fancy goods, you can afford to pay the rent. You've heard from my solicitor, so he tells me. That's your final warning. Settle, or you're out!'

With that, he drove off; the sheep on the back of his pickup staring like a bunch of small-town jurors whose silence was their assent.

Wednesday

Still no sign of any cheque.

I've begun to wonder if the postman does anything more than deliver the missives from Williams as ordered by Voyle.

With no great pleasure, I've found myself contemplating the kind of man Williams might be. I think of him as lean and bony, curt and clean-shaven, cut-glass and cut-throat, like the worst of his profession. There'll be no point in me making any appeal to him.

Somehow, though, I *must* call-in a favour.

Here, on this coast, a cell phone is a perfectly useless thing: we are too removed, too shadowed, too 'sunk down' by the sea.

And so, shortly before midday, I

walked to the red phone box that stands by a road (on which I've never seen a car) in open country a mile from here.

In a strange way, its scarlet cubicle – I've visited it before – is a sanctuary. It's warm in there – glasshouse-warm – even on days of tepid, winter sun.

The phone is an old one with a circular dial. It gives out whirs, clicks and, then, 'pips'... to summon coins, before it will connect you.

Previously, I've felt (perhaps hoped) – while pushing my money into its slot – that it might somehow re-route me: transferring my call to a number from the past. That my father, for example, will pick it up at the other end, in some earlier decade, where he's come in from the garden, having been mowing the lawn... that, after some words with him about college and rugby, he'll pass me to my mother who has, likewise, left her summer house (full of plants and books), having heard the ringing across the newly-striped grass.

Eventually, after repeated instructions to 'Hold, please', I reached my editor's secretary.

'I need—' I said.

And then my coins ran out.

As I stepped from the box, its iron door fell shut, with a sound and air of heavy finality.

On my way back to the cottage – keen not to return to its 'comforts' too soon – I went down to the beach.

In the strandline, on a clump of dry bladderwrack that had the thickly thatched look of a heron's nest, I saw a pair of glasses... of the old-fashioned kind: one round lens broken, the other intact... slightly dusted with sand and yet catching the sun and – via several sharp glints – also my eyes.

I reached down to the weed and picked them up.

Absurd as this may sound, I put them on, wrapping the brass wire ends around my ears.

And what strange scenes I saw... or thought that I did (I'm still not sure which).

Till then, the beach had been its usual calm, even desolate, self.

Now – suddenly – it was a very *different* shore: consumed with the crashing of waves, the shooting of sea spray, the shrieking of seabirds, and the most tremendous 'roar'.

Amid all this were pitiful screams and cries.

Through my lenses, dark shapes... *human* shapes, washed to and fro – lifeless – in the foaming water.

Much nearer me (their forms no more than blurs due to the distortion of 'my' glasses), figures hurried down to the shore... and then doubled back to the high shingle and cliffs.

I heard their shouts and, unless I'm mistaken, felt one of their number brush against me as he ran.

Having seen all this (in mere moments), I tore the spectacles from my eyes and ears.

And I stood there: fearful, breathless, head spinning, my heart pounding in my chest.

When, finally, I had composed myself I saw that the beach was as quiet and empty as it had ever been.

I was utterly alone.

In time, I turned and set off, back to the cottage, wondering about this weird 'waking dream' that I'd witnessed.

Without knowing it – just as I might have with my own glasses after giving a reading somewhere... to faint, polite applause in an almost-empty room – I put the spectacles in a side pocket of my jacket as I went.

Thursday

After breakfast, I took to the cliffs. I was – after the unsettling sights of the beach – disinclined to comb it for a while. A stroll along the clifftops, I thought, might help me clear my head.

The thumb stick – which has become quite a companion – saw me safely over walls and stiles, its shaft reaching out and planting itself firmly in the ground ahead.

I ought to have guessed – from the neglected nature of the boundaries that I crossed – that the land that I was on was Voyle's.

And, in time, I saw him.

He was amid some cows in a field inland from the one through which I was passing, with the sea to my right.

I half expected him to come bounding towards me... to at least shout some abuse.

Yet he kept his distance and his silence.

All he did was eye me (with a reserve that I found puzzling) as I continued on my way.

Having walked for the best of two hours, I judged it time to turn back.

I sensed it wise not to return via the route by which I had come, thinking that Voyle – never mind his previous hesitancy – might have something unpleasant in store.

I therefore made my way to what seemed the lowest and most benign of the cliffs, and clambered down its face.

Near the bottom, having slid over some scree, I put out my right hand to stop myself from upending (my left hand held on to my stick).

Doing so, I felt my open palm fall on something on the top of a large rock, at that point where the cliff rose from the piled pebbles of the upper shore.

Instinctively, my hand grasped whatever it was.

On my feet, on the beach, I opened it... and saw an old, clay pipe – intact save for what seemed a small portion snapped from the top end of its slender stem.

I took it for the type a sailor might once have smoked: light in weight and very white (the sun had been on it for some long while, no doubt). It was like a piece of bone.

Oddly, to me at least, there was a distinct charring... a blackening... inside its bowl. It was as if – never mind its age (at least a hundred years, I supposed) – it had been smoked by some Jack Tar that very same day.

During my walk back to the cottage, I saw no sign of Voyle – or any other soul.

The day had been a clear one, and the air – by this hour – was turning cold.

I placed the pipe on the mantelpiece in the parlour, as I made a small fire with a handful of coals.

Friday

This morning, the strangest thing.

Unless my senses are deceiving me: the smell of tobacco smoke in the downstairs rooms of the cottage. I've never touched the stuff: I know it cannot have come from me. And it can't have been the fire, whose coals burned out long before I went to bed. The aroma of tobacco is different, anyway.

And there was more. On the kitchen table, beside my notes and papers, where I had – after a fashion – been reading and editing before fatigue overtook me, lay the glasses... the ones from the beach. Meanwhile, against the wooden kitchen chair, rested the thumb stick (which I felt sure I had left in the porch).

It was as if someone had entered 'my' cottage and made themselves at home.

I dismissed this as impossible. I must have been responsible, I told myself. Or even Voyle, who, as the landlord, surely has a key.

Part of me considers him too stupid for such mind games. Yet some country people have a slyness: you underestimate them at your peril.

Disregarding the violence that I felt sure boiled within him, I resolved to pay Voyle a visit. My idea: to see if he might grant me the grace of a week or three (until a cheque – I hope – comes through).

His farm is a grim and gloomy place. The house lurks on a low hill overlooking his land. It's an ugly old fort of a thing: irregular windows set in high walls washed with an ancient and grimed grey paint, its ramparts suppurating slime in green and black trails.

The main building squats at the top of a long, private track. Had a rapacious Norman knight been looking for a spot to plant a keep, he would surely have picked that brow.

Walking the unkempt lane, I swear I heard the ringing of a phone. Not from the farm but, so it seemed, to my mind and ears, the box I'd used those days before.

I stopped and listened.

I wondered if the ringing was for me: someone calling – at last – with news of a payment – or even a gift – which they were putting in the post.

The sound died.

Some lapwings rose and fell in a field beside the track, as if they also had been uneased.

I walked on.

When I finally reached it, Voyle's yard lay quiet. No onrushing dogs. No scattering, squawking hens.

What struck me was the *un*farm-like nature of the place. In truth, its old, cobbled courtyard was more like that of a chandler's, or shipwright's.

A mermaid, in the form of a figurehead from a ship, leaned out – as if to greet me – from a mossed stone wall, her carved shape once strikingly colourful, I didn't doubt, but now worn, wormed and flaking.

Around me, nautical paraphernalia of all kinds rested and nested: great copper-cased lanterns; huge iron anchors; tree-like lengths of dark, rounded timber that could only have been masts; wooden casks with metal hoops; rope of the coarse and tarred type; old floats – ball-

like and made of glass – strung and in stacks.

As I neared what I took to be Voyle's door, I saw a small, wheeled cannon – from Nelson's time, by its looks – 'on guard' at his step.

When I finally rang, it was a ship's bell that I sounded with my hand.

Even the door at which I stood had the appearance of a panel prised from some vessel of yore. A serpent with a staring eye swam through its mouldering board.

And yet – from what I knew – the master of that place had never been to sea... had never left dry land. (Nor – it was apparent to me – was he much of a farmer.)

There were – maybe still are – wreckers here... on this coast: looters, plunderers, pirates, call them what you will: people, whole families in fact, who – with lanterns and false signals – drew ships onto the rocks. And when the poor passengers and crew were washed ashore, those human vultures stripped them of whatever they could get... however they could get it – be their victims alive and begging for help... or dead, in the surf's cold embrace.

The heirs to those who partook in

the frenzied cutting-off of ring fingers, the rifling of pockets, the snatching of necklaces, the stealing of teeth, ignoring all pleas for pity... not to mention the carrying away of all manner of cargo: tea, wine, spirits, spices, salt – anything and everything that their greedy hands might grasp... *they* survive, of course. While I do not judge them for the actions of their ancestors, the past is never far away in an old – and outwardly quiet – crack in the coast such as this.

The door in front of me opened. Not fully. Perhaps to a gap of three inches.

Voyle showed himself – in part.

Although I could see no more than a narrow length of him, his manner was very different from the brute who'd banged my door: his belligerence gone, replaced with an air not merely of caution, but, I sensed, concern.

I remembered his conduct in the field with the cattle: the fact that he hadn't shouted or waved a fist.

He seemed... haunted.

When I told him I needed more time to pay the rent, my words scarcely seemed to register.

He interrupted me before I'd uttered much more than a sentence: the awful sourness of his breath causing me to hold my own.

What he wanted to know was whether I'd gone there 'alone'.

He began talking nonsensically: of there being 'someone else' in my cottage, and how, apart from anything, this was a breach of my lease.

For a moment, he seemed to look over my shoulder.

Looking back at me, he said he'd seen 'him' – in my cottage, crossing the fields, doing as 'he' damned well pleased.

Voyle snatched the door so that its edge stood a mere inch from the jamb.

All I saw now was a bloodshot eye and a corner of his crooked mouth.

Sweat – which seemed to me of the feverous kind – beaded a band of his part-shadowed cheek.

He wasn't interested in what I had to say, he told me. All he wanted was me *out*. Gone! And *never* to come back!

He shut the door. I heard him drive home its bolts then retreat from its timber: listening for me... wondering, so it seemed, in the gloom of his hall – his heavy, panting breath audible through the door's dark wood.

Walking back down the track, I found myself wondering if my landlord was a madman, as well as a monster.

Not for the first time after an encounter with him, I felt the need to cleanse myself, and made for the beach.

I sank my hands in the cold shallows of a rockpool. This act made me think of those stone stoups of holy water that can be found in the porches of churches of certain faiths.

My eyes examined the world within the rockpool's basin.

Not far from my fingers, I noticed – among a bed of anemones and bottle-green weed – something strange and circular, about the size of a large coin of the kind that are no longer minted.

I reached for it with my right hand and drew it out.

Rising from my crouch, I studied the object.

It was the blackened case of an old pocket watch: the remains... the *ruin* of a timepiece, it might be said.

Its face and mechanism – the wheels, screws and springs – were entirely missing. What was left, in my hands, was the back panel, the circumference – for want of the correct term – and the winder at the top.

Its innards, I judged, had been dashed out – years, decades, maybe even centuries earlier – in some cruel collision on that same shore.

I stowed it in my trouser pocket.

A breeze of some strength swept over

the beach, corrugating the surface of the pool.

I saw that the sky was darkening, that foam was cresting the water in the bay, and that there was every prospect of a storm.

I set off quickly for the relative shelter of the cottage.

***

Writing this now, as I am, in a state of bewilderment, with dawn mercifully breaking around me, I can say – *swear* – that *never* have I found myself caught in such a tempest as the one that – somehow – I seem to have survived.

I had been home here for no more than half an hour when – in all its malign magnificence – the storm erupted: slates flying from the roof of the cottage, as if they were mere paper sheets, one almost taking my head off as, early in the onslaught, I went outside to inspect the damage. From that moment on, all was madness. The night raged around me like a tyrant... howled like the most tortured of souls. Panes of glass cracked and splintered in their frames, three of them shattering and blowing-in entirely. At least one of the chimneys has come down. The gate has surely been smashed to matchwood; the wilderness of the garden churned and in large part washed away. How the walls withstood it, I shall never know, but I thank God that they did.

And yet, the most peculiar aspect... the weirdest thing, that I now bring to mind, here, in the eerie silence of the aftermath, is this: before the cyclone, I heard – from the parlour (where I had left that ruined timepiece from the rockpool) – steady and precise as you like – a tick, tick, ticking.

Saturday
Strangely, on this day of my intended eviction... the one on which I was supposed to pay up or 'walk the plank', I've heard

and seen (beyond the savage damage of the storm)... nothing.

Of Voyle and Williams, not a sign.

In the case of the latter, perhaps that's not much of a surprise. Solicitors seldom care to concern themselves with the consequences of their letters: far better to dispatch a gang of roughnecks to deal with any dirty work.

But Voyle?

His no-show *has* been a shock. I thought he would have been here – surveying the wreckage of his property, picking through it, blaming me ('I *told* you so! Didn't I?!'), rooting... grunting, like some bad-tempered boar.

It seems I've won a reprieve. The tide has turned. Or else, something has... blown in on it.

I shall celebrate with a walk.

I did think the thumb stick was in the parlour. But I have seen it, just now, in the porch – as if it has already been out... swinging... beating, on business of its own.

Its shaft feels somehow... slick... almost *oiled*. Not with rain, or even seawater, but with something... thicker, something... darker.

It has about it a smell that – to *my* nose – is rather sweet.

The two of us shall venture out soon. The morning is still moody, but the sun is doing her best: eyelets of light breaching a curtain of sky that has the colour of a heavy bruise... of the black and bloody kind.

Wreck as it unquestionably is, I don't think I shall quit my tenancy of Crab Cottage just yet.

Like the 'V' of my thumb stick, it seems to have me – *us* – in its claw.

I shall stick here for a while, I suspect... and see what the tide brings in.

THE KEEPING OF PEARLS

by Janice Leadingham

*T*he psychic told me *to get a cat. She held my palm in her oily hands, as slick and familiar as lovers. She traced the lines of my heart and life with the soft pad of her fingertip.*

'Get a cat.'

She laid my hand down on the green felt table, patted it gently, and pulled a packet of French fries out of her pocket, grease bled through the crinkly, white bag.

'Why?' I asked.

She shrugged and ate a fry.

The shelter's cages were full. Litter box dust floated in the air and the punch of ammonia stung my nose and watered my eyes. I had a string of orange tabbies growing up – always named Red or Tiger or something. To anyone else, it looked like the same cat stalking blue jays in the front yard for 18 years or so. A plastic placard tied to his cage called him Precious. Precious was shades of orange all over but the tip of his tail was bone bright, the insides of his ears and his toes were the pink of healthy gums and in the centre of his nose, as cool and wet as a sweating milk jug, a black freckle as declarative as a period. He was fully grown, though he had done this growing outside of the shelter and so his precise age was a mystery. A cousin to the ones that came before him, I called him Cousin.

The house stood, white as copy paper, its milky face broken up only by the tidy blue shutters and matching blue door, on the intersecting corners of two streets, both named for flowers. It had two bed-rooms, one downstairs and one upstairs in what used to be the attic. A stone path led to the front door and was flanked on both sides with anatomically-pink roses that smelled like pepper and lemon, and in the springtime, drunk bees napped in the folds of the petals in the afternoon. On winter days, a newer furnace pumped warm air throughout the limbs of the house and the old wood bones creaked and settled, con-tent. Cold faceted-cut glass doorknobs that never warmed from human touch bejew-eled every door in the house, even that of the broom closet – in my periphery, they were diamonds dangling from the blushed earlobes of debutantes. The heels of my most-responsible looking shoes click-clacked on the wide-plank wood floors when I made the waltz from living room, to dining room, to kitchen, and back.

When I moved in, the neighbour across the street in the Cape Cod brought over a bottle of wine. Her eyes were round, the whites porcelain bright but with veins cracked through them and, on her left arm, moles trailed out of her pink gingham short shirt sleeve like ants at a picnic. I re-member that she talked about the woman who lived in the house before me, although I didn't care. I know that she mentioned the teacups because I thought, 'Oh, that explains the teacups.' And I know she said, 'Well, the whole neighborhood got togeth-er to buy her stone.' And I looked confused and she said, 'The tombstone, you know.'

It happened first in the kitchen. I made toast and coffee, the toast on the chi-na plate with painted roses, the coffee in one of the teacups – and ate it standing at the counter. With the last bite, I brushed the crumbs onto the floor and wiped my hands on my cotton nightgown.

And then – the crash. Or, multiple crashes really, like rocks crashing through the roof or maybe bowling balls bouncing down an alley.

I stood still in the sort of silence that comes with saying something you can't take back and waited for the walls to cave in on me.

In the hallway, the door to the broom closet stood open, the bare light bulb blinked on and off and on, and the broom and dustpan splayed out on the wood floor. I picked them up, the house still silent apart from the soft pad-swoosh-pad of my slippers, and swept up the crumbs and emptied the pan into the bin. I scrubbed the plate with violet-scented dish soap and sat it in the drying rack and reached for the teacup and emptied it into the sink. Something hard and small slipped out of the coffee and hit the bottom of the old enamel sink with an assertive ping. I picked it up and rinsed it off. A pearl.

***

The groundskeeper told me, 'There is a shelf-life on grief, visit any cemetery and you'll see.'

I nodded, wishing I didn't need his guidance. He found me twirling at the gate, hoping to ping my internal North.

He said, 'Give it two or three genera-tions and there's no one left to care.'

He pointed to a ring of stones sticking out of the ground like they belonged to it, mushrooms in the forest. His hands were bloated red and bruised purple and the unders of his nails were stained grassy green.

Corpse hands, corpse hands, my thoughts sang.

I assumed it would be tricky, looking for the grave of the person that haunted my house. I told him what I knew about the neighbours buying a stone for an old lady and it was, somehow, enough.

We walked together, grass sticking to

my shoes with dew. A diner abutted the outside of the far gate, beside the crematorium, and the cemetery air smelled like summer camp. My stomach growled.

He stopped at a stone and stroked the moss spreading over its curved edges, rounded from weather like old mountain tops.

Corpse hands, corpse hands.

'You found her,' he said. I stood to his left, right on top of

Martha Norman

No dates, no life line. The stone stood clean and stark, its corners still military sharp. There were no affectations, she wasn't a 'loving mother' or 'caring wife'. Not even a 'cherished daughter'. My feet sank into the soft ground of her. A pinwheel on the grave next-door spun panic-rapid in the breeze.

The groundskeeper clumped grass off her grave and ran it through his fingers like hair, the tendrils blowing in the meat-cooking breeze. He pulled a hard-boiled egg out of his pocket and rolled it over the top of her stone, the shell cracking until he could get to the soft innards turned grassy green from his corpse-y fingers.

I thanked him and asked how to leave.

He stuffed the egg, whole, into his mouth.

Muffled through sulphuric, ovum breaths he said, 'The entrance and the exit are the same.'

***

I didn't own a spirit board or long white tapered candles or a gazing ball or anything, but I did have a nearly complete set of pink, puffy alphabet & numerical refrigerator magnets. The night of the day that began with a pearl, I decided to start a conversation with Martha. It took me a little while to collect all the letters, my mind and hands sluggish from the wine I sipped from a jam jar. I flipped a M into a W and

subbed 0 for O.

WHAT D0 YOU WANT ?

I finished my jar of wine and sat it in the sink and went off to bed.

The next morning, I woke up with a headache and a soured stomach. And then I remembered clicking the magnetic letters into place on the fridge. An excited thunderstorm roiled in my gut. I tip-toed past the tattle-tale floorboards of the living room, as if I could scare off a reply from the thing rattling my broom closet. Pink letters littered the ground. The rest still stuck to the fridge read:

W A   YOU   T

***

I visited the psychic some years before she told me to get a cat. She assured me that I didn't have a STI and the doctor confirmed as much a few months later, so, when I asked her about Martha and she told me to get a cat, I did. And she was right again.

It is much easier to explain away noises in the night when you have a cat. 'Oh, it's just the cat,' you say, as you sink deeper into your pillow.

Cousin moved in, easy. He took over the left side of the couch by the window, a melted creamsicle in the sun. He watched the squirrels in the maple tree and the drowsy bees by the roses. He snuggled with me in bed at night, all warm and tuna-scented, and woke me with sweet fuzzy nuzzles in the morning. I taught him to rattle a closed door when he wanted in or out. I said, 'knock' and rattled the door to show him. I gave him turkey-flavoured treats from the expensive grocery store.

Those first few weeks with Cousin, Martha was quiet. She didn't answer my puffy-pink questions, she didn't scare me with loud noises, or reward me with jewels or trinkets. But I felt her growing warmer, sunlight cracking through the curtains.

One night, Cousin woke me knocking on the bedroom door to be let out. I opened it for him and said, 'Good boy!' He rubbed his wide head on my calf in thanks and I flung my body back into the bed. Cousin rattled the door again. I got up to let him back in, but he was knocking on the door to the broom closet.

RAP- RAP- RAP.

'COUSIN,' I called down the hall.

RAP-RAP-RAP.

He stood with his ear to the crack of the door, listening. Secret telling.

My feet crept me closer. A lullaby of whispers came from behind the broom closet door, the words shh-shh-shhed together so that I couldn't pick them apart. Cousin head-butted the door, and rubbed his wide body on it, purring in tune with the rhythmic whispers.

'Martha?' I asked.

***

Cousin brought gifts. For Martha. Crickets and spiders, living and dead. Leftover kibble from his bowl. My hair ties. Always presented the same way, to the bottom crack of the door to Martha's broom closet. I got up one night to pee and my left foot squelched on something warm and soggy. I slipped and landed hard on my hip. I laid there for a minute, taking in the pain and the wet that splattered up my bare leg from the bottom of my foot. The sliver of light from the crack of my bedroom door projected on the fresh gore of tiny, recently-pulsating organs stuck slick to my leg with what I could only guess (hope) was mouse juice. Cousin slinked towards me in the hall and meowed his concern with fishy breath into my face. I think that was the only time I ever yelled at him.

Martha loved the gifts, she was angry with me whenever I cleaned them up – she could abide by Cousin's mess. After

I yelled at Cousin and mopped up the gutted mouse, Martha was so mad at me that she froze me out. Really. Paranormal investigators talk about cold spots on TV and they shudder and puff out foggy breaths into the air, but I know they've never actually experienced one because they are painful. Unable to bend your fingers or wiggle your toes, a preview of empty veins.

When Martha was especially pleased with my performance as Cousin's caretaker, she would treat me with messages on the fridge, doing her best with the limited letters. They were never sweet notes or anything, but she would let me know the furnace needed repair or that a family of squirrels was trying to nest in the crawl space. Or that my lipstick was too orange for my complexion.

Ghosts and cats both get the zoomies the moment you slip into REM. This is an almost biological fact. This is the hunting hour, the witching hour, the most primal parts of beasts know this time by the way the beats slow in your chest.

And that time belonged to them.

Sort of.

To be awakened at midnight by your cat playing fetch with a ghost and a necklace worth of loose pearls is to be a reluctant participant. However much I hated the mean parent role, at least they were including me.

***

Cousin died late one night, still curled up beside me with his arms out midstretch and his eyes closed. We were together long enough for his ruddy, pumpkin face to ashen, and the first steps of crows-feet to creep beneath my eyes. He wasn't sick and I didn't know it was coming, but it did anyway. I stayed with him in bed until I knew it was real. I buried him in the backyard and planted a blanket of nasturtiums and poppies to cover him.

Martha had to have known, but she was quiet. I needed her in that moment, to ask her, is he with you?

I couldn't ask the psychic, she had started a daycare centre.

So, I yelled at Martha. At her broom closet. And I said, 'I did my best!' and 'I loved him too!'. I stomped into the kitchen and tore open drawers and banged them closed and opened the cabinet doors and slammed them closed and opened up all the canisters on the countertop and smashed their lids down.

I made a pot of coffee.

I stared at the teacup, watching the liquid lose its steam. I wanted to ask her, why do some stay and some leave?

I drank my coffee in one gulp – but there was something else. Something hard and small slipped over my tongue and stuck itself into my throat as though it had thorns. I coughed and coughed and my throat was briars but I still couldn't catch the wisp of a breath. The teacup fell to shatters on the floor, the little porcelain pieces like teeth in a growing-up smile. I dropped to my hands and knees, the shards shredding my skin, and I couldn't breathe, I couldn't breathe, I couldn't breathe. I clawed at my throat, trying to rip the barb out with my fingernails. My chest downhill caved.

As my vision blotted over with ink, I looked over to the fridge. Spelled out in the remaining letters, a final message from Martha

W AY OUT

***

The psychic looked annoyed. I watched her watching the kids kick up dirt storms as they ran around the backyard. The dust settled onto the jam and oatmeal and other sticky bits on their baby bodies.

'Gross,' I said.

The psychic rolled her eyes and took a deep drag from her cigarette.

I told her I still dream and when I do my hands search the pockets of my most sensible coat and find only sand where there should've been pearls.

She said, 'The thing about pearls is they lose their sheen if you don't wear them. Something about skin and warmth keeps 'em shiny.'

'Was it a pearl?' I asked.

She shrugged and knocked the ash from her cigarette into the lip of a soda can.

THE FIREMAN

by Verity Holloway

T he Anvil has been anchored *off Majorca for a week and a day. None may go ashore and none may board us. It is not a physician's place to speak charitably of superstition. I break this personal imperative only to log my interactions with a patient of mine: one Mister Sheppard, a stoker aboard this vessel.*

The dissection of the unexplained, I believe, is the scientist's anchor. Like inclement weather, the inexplicable may take many forms, and what may begin as a spatter of rain is liable to become a typhoon in an instant. In climates such as these we must hold fast, with all the cool-headed dignity we can muster.

Nevertheless, I am resolved to burn these pages.

Able Seaman Sheppard. 32 years of age. A Norfolk man, and a lifelong sailor. A glance at his records show the complaints one would expect from a man who shovels coal all day: minor burns and lacerations, one amputated toe. Nothing to suggest an unsound mind.

Sheppard first came to the infirmary on the morning of the eighteenth of July, 1883. We had left Portsmouth some eight weeks prior, touring the usual spots, with no action. An ironclad vessel has no need to show its strength. The mere presence of the Anvil scatters all foes to the wind. That morning, we were cruising along the coast of Portugal, allowing the sails to do most of the work.

My young assistant, Mister Harris, ushered Sheppard in with the customary crustiness which endears him to no one but me. Sheppard loitered, eyeing the cabinets of bottles with their impenetrable Latin labels. Harris knew the man in passing. He was a sociable fellow, Harris told me, known amongst the men as something of a humourist, and I took his reticence to mean he had some embarrassing ailment of the nether regions. I was about to reassure him, as I did all the men, that I spend my life examining the private parts of sailors and find them quite tedious, but something in Sheppard's face stayed my tongue.

The stokers are envied and pitied in equal measure. These men are paid more than regular seaman, another half in fact, and are provided with baths and good soap for when they come off watch. But the poor souls work in Hell. I have seen these men cough up chunks of foaming black matter and take no notice. Eight-hundred-and-fifty tonnes of coal won't be mastered without a fight, but they must do so, in white uniforms.

To my surprise, Sheppard required a sleeping draught.

Though it is unusual for a stoker to struggle to rest, even surrounded by his snoring crewmates, it is not unheard of. I furnished Sheppard with a mild opiate and instructed him to take three drops in water before settling into his hammock. He thanked me, nodded to Harris, who ignored him, and returned to the engine room.

The Anvil was somewhere off Lisbon, I believe, when Sheppard returned. He was sour with perspiration, as was I. We were caught in an unusually hot pocket of weather. The wind had fallen and en-gines were on full steam. Harris was more short-tempered than usual, to my personal amusement.

'If you still can't sleep, don't consider yourself part of a select club,' Harris said.

The stoker stood in the infirmary doorway, cap in hand. He looked haggard – indeed more nervous than before, as if this time I might prescribe the knife. 'Begging your pardon, sir. It's been days.'

'Very well. Let's take a look at you. Are you in pain?'

As I waved him over, Sheppard was muscled out of the way by a young sailor in a state of agitation. 'Sir! Sir, someone's come a'cropper.'

Harris was up and handing me my bag before the man could finish his sentence.

It was Harold Walsh, one of our young rawbones. I drew up the death certificate: born 1864, died 1883. It appears he fell afoul of the steep ladder leading down to the engine room. A superficial autopsy revealed no obvious alcohol consumption. Sweaty palms slipping on the handrails, I imagine. No one saw him fall. If he did not die instantly, I wrote in the log, he did so wretchedly alone.

The Anvil chugged on unchallenged. The officers spoke of boredom and passed the time by handing out floggings to any man without pristine uniform. I thought with sympathy of the stokers, heaving and sweating down in the engine room in their stiff white cotton. I had forgotten Sheppard entirely.

August brought further misfortune. One afternoon, Harris and I were preparing to treat a lad with a broken femur, so I confess I took little notice of Sheppard's demeanour when he interrupted us. Nevertheless, he would not leave until I gave him another sleeping draught.

The break was a bad one. We had no choice but to amputate.

'It's alright, McDowell. We have chloroform,' I told him, smiling so the lad would think I hadn't seen the tears in his eyes. 'And you aren't my first.'

Harris made a face as we washed our hands. 'Someone ought to do something about those ladders. He must have gone down like a cannonball to snap a bone like that.'

Out of McDowell's sight, Harris opened the case of saws and forceps. He offered me a tight smile. He knew I hated the business of butchery, and I was grateful for his concern.

'Ash on my kit,' McDowell snivelled as Harris held him down. 'They'll hang me.'

'Even our captain wouldn't hang a man for a smut on a sleeve,' Harris said, smoothing McDowell's hair from his eyes.

But McDowell was delirious with pain. 'Everyone—will—know.'

I covered the patient's nose and mouth with the ether mask, and set my mind to my grisly task.

***

At a quarter past two, I was awoken. Despite bathing, I reeked of another man's blood, and a hot wave of it turned my stomach. Someone was banging on the cabin door. Harris swore as he slithered out of bed. He didn't bother to don shoes or jacket.

Sheppard, wheezing like a locomotive, had been dragged to the infirmary by a pair of sailors. He was keeping them awake, they said. There was something wrong with him.

I peeled back the stoker's eyelids to see blood vessels like a map of the tides. 'Is he drunk?'

'We tried that, sir. Nothing calms him. Look.'

The sailor snatched up Sheppard's calloused hand. The thumbnail was prised from its bed like an oyster shell.

'He's using splinters from the deck. Shoving them up there, the great pillock.'

'Sheppard? Will you speak to me?'

But the stoker was staring over my shoulder, at the aprons we'd hung up to dry after working on McDowell. I had

thought them clean, but in the lamplight they were rusty and stiff with blood. Sheppard gave a low wail. When the other sailors tightened their grip, he lashed out.

'McDowell's his mate,' said one man. 'Not taking his death well.'

Harris yawned. 'He isn't dead. A little lighter, but he'll keep.'

I judged it the sensible thing to say. I was mistaken.

It took both sailors, Harris and myself to prevent Sheppard from dashing out his brains against the wall.

I was panting as we pinned his flailing limbs to the deck. 'Sheppard, I don't want to restrain you, but you leave me little choice.'

'Everyone will know.' He wasn't talking to me. He stared up at our swinging aprons with shining eyes.

'Know what?' I said.

I was glad of Harris at my side as we strapped him into bed.

***

A more stifling night I could not imagine. I dreamt of fire, of the Hell below me in the engine room. Men in ashen uniforms peeling them away along with their skin, hanging them up to dry like the aprons in the infirmary.

I can generally rely on Harris to wake me with coffee and a modicum of gruff sympathy. That morning, though, he was otherwise engaged.

Through the cabin wall I heard him holler my name – wreathed in blasphemy – and I sprang up, stumbling half-dressed into the infirmary.

Even now I can scarcely believe what I saw. As Harris raised the alarm, I checked the supply cabinets. Locked, just as I left them. All surgical implements were accounted for. McDowell's sickbed was rumpled, but empty. Our patient was gone.

I shook Sheppard, sprawled in the adjacent bunk. 'Did you see him go?'

He rubbed at his eyes with sooty

knuckles. 'I slept,' he said, and with alarm, I realised his restraints were unbuckled.

'Mister Harris,' he explained. 'In the night. Said he hated seeing a man strung up like a bit of gammon.'

I paced the room. It made no sense. New amputees don't hoist themselves up and go for a stroll. For one thing, I had left McDowell no crutches. We had given Sheppard enough opium to fell an elephant; even if he had seen something, he would never remember it.

***

Need I say the search for McDowell was futile? Harris and I were not at liberty to join the hunt. Three men were admitted with sickness and diarrhea, which is no laughing matter in an enclosed space. My day was spent administering fluids and dodging spillages, cursing the heat and the stench with every breath. Harris was all too pleased to shoo Sheppard back to work with a few choice words about malingering. The stoker was pale, but satisfactorily improved, I thought, for the rest.

Harris and I took our supper on deck that night, looking out at the sultry lights of Cadiz. In all our years working within inches of one another, I had come to know his ways in microscopic detail, and he mine. There is power in intimate companionship. Our communication, like that of twins, was largely silent.

I was not surprised when, after cajoling me into forcing down some buttered bread, Harris spoke of McDowell. 'Could he have pitched himself overboard?'

'It's possible. The loss of a limb can drive men to it.'

There was no need to voice my thoughts about the ladders he would have to climb, drained and dressed as he was, like a lamb in a butcher's window. Neither was I prepared to speak of my feelings, half-formed and slippery in the muggy night air. But Harris knew. Our thoughts are made of similar tissue.

'I've displeased you.'

'No,' I said, glad to stop short of *never*. 'You are indispensable. I only... I must know I can depend on you. Setting Sheppard loose like that. You ought to have asked.'

Harris's face screwed into an amused grimace. 'The man was delirious. I wouldn't set him loose any more than I'd let a bull run about the place. You're cracked, old man. You haven't had a decent night's sleep in weeks. You'll have untied him and forgotten.' He looked into his tea, swirled it around in the cup. The distant city of Cadiz reflected in his eyes, an uneasy glimmer. 'Just... watch yourself.'

'Whatever do you mean?'

Harris patted my arm. 'I'll fetch us something stronger.'

***

The heat of Cadiz was more hateful than that of Portugal. I was tempted to take one of my own sleeping draughts. I dreamt of the blue spectre of cholera, of decks awash with blood and effluvia. They took me to the engine room, those dreams, a roiling pit of smoke. Stokers crept about like damned souls hoping not to be singled out by the Devil's knowing eyes. The utter nakedness of the dissecting table. All secrets revealed. I thrashed in my bunk, searching for the exit. I wasn't a stoker. I wasn't like them. I hadn't *done* anything.

I woke with a yell when Harris threw a pillow at me.

No cholera, thank God. My patients had consumed some bad salt beef. The Anvil powered on around the south of Spain, unchallenged, alone.

When I heard the tentative knock, I did not have to look up from my ledgers.

'Come in, Sheppard. How are the fingernails?'

'You been expecting me, sir?'

'I am a doctor, Sheppard. I have seen every fleshly horror you can imagine...' I spoke as gently as I could. Still, his shoulders stiffened. I went on: '...but few things rattle me like a man on the brink of addiction.'

'Sir?'

'First begging for a sleeping draught, then these strange commotions. You've been fighting it, but you need it now, don't you?'

His hair was lank with sweat. Curiously, when he shook his head, I could see he meant it.

I bid him sit, taking note of his trembling hands. A sure sign of dependence. 'You knew McDowell, didn't you? You were mates.'

He scratched at a smear of pale ash on his cheek. 'You got that secrecy, haven't you? You doctors. Like priests.'

I assured him confidentiality was my watchword.

He pondered this for some time. 'I liked McDowell,' he said quietly. 'He was a good sort.'

'And Walsh?'

'He had a... an agreeable singing voice.' Sheppard's damp throat worked through a swallow. 'I liked his songs.'

'One friend dead. And another, most likely. You're grieving, man. It will pass. But the second you turn to opium, or to drink...'

I must have said something foolish. Sheppard interrupted me, unexpectedly intense: 'You ever been down in the engine room?'

'I admit, I take care not to.'

'I've been a stoker since I were fifteen. Hard work. But good. Work like that don't give you time for brewing things over. You got your work and you got your mates and that's your lot. You follow me?'

I did, in my own way. But Sheppard's force alarmed me.

'I was all alright 'til I saw him sitting there.'

At this, my eyes flicked up. 'Sitting? On duty?'

The stoker gave an unpleasant laugh. 'He has his own idea of duty, sir.'

'Look here, Sheppard, you don't have to give me a name, but there are strict protocols for a reason. Someone could die.'

He rubbed his dirty cheek. I fancied the ash sat beneath the dermis somehow, like the tattooed sailors of Singapore Harris spoke of in tones of awe.

'Sheppard, tell me. Did McDowell neglect his duty? Or Walsh?'

'He isn't one of us.'

'You're not making sense, man.'

'He sits *inside* the furnace.'

Sheppard as good as bellowed it at me.

On examination, his eyes were bloodshot but responsive to light, his pulse thready but nothing to be concerned about. I palpated his liver: no enlargement. No immediate sign of venereal disease. He was hot, but weren't we all?

'We all see things in the flames,' he said, having wrestled back his composure. 'Down there in the dark all day, you see all sorts dancing about. Usually it's horses, for me, galloping and gone. A lot see faces, but—' Sheppard met my eyes and held them fast. 'There was a man. Sitting. Inside the furnace.'

'Was?' I contained my scepticism. A nervous invalid must be met with compassion, not scorn. 'He's gone now?'

'It's worse when he's gone.'

'Describe him to me.'

'You know what a man looks like, sir.'

'A man impervious to flame.' Perhaps repeating it would bring him to his senses. But I suspected Sheppard was beyond the reach of logic.

'He watches me,' he said. 'When I feed the boiler. He's there when I come on duty and stays right through till the end of my shift. He don't bother no one else.'

'And why is that?'

'I can't say.'

'You don't know?'

'I cannot *say*.'

He feared this man. I did not insult him by acknowledging it.

'You said it's worse when he isn't in the flames. Why is that?'

'He goes a'wandering. He comes up to the gundeck now, when we're sleeping. I see his footprints in ash, all around the hammocks. He likes the ones who talk. In their sleep, like.' He stiffened at a noise; only Harris bumping around in our cabin next door. 'McDowell was a talker.'

'And you want sleep. Sleep so deeply you don't know if this phantom is there or not.'

'I did want that. But now he gets inside. I'll be dreaming of my mother and my sister at the dinner table in Cromer, and I'll be passing the beer jug to Mary and then he's sitting there, smouldering like a side of roast mutton.' Sheppard placed his head in his hands. 'And then he opens his mouth...'

I do not relish the sight of a crying man. I recommended Sheppard be placed on light duties until his condition improved. No sense having a nervous sailor in the engine room. As I said, someone could die.

***

In the week following this disquieting exchange, more men complained of cramps and fever. I administered purgatives, fasting them until the invading force was starved out. I kept a close eye on Harris in case the contagion should touch him. Sheppard was right about one thing; you have your work and you have your mates, and that is enough.

The Anvil was buffeted like a toy in a tin bath as the heat converged into thick cloud and a spiteful wind.

When one is on duty, a storm is the enemy to be fought and overcome. But to lie there and helplessly endure is a torment for any sailor. Doubled up on his bunk, one of my patients – a softly-spoken young steward – trembled head to toe. I went to him without thinking, knelt down, and gave his hand a heartening squeeze.

The ship moaned as a hard wave caught us portside. There came a wheezing laugh behind us. My patient jerked his hand away and I turned, surprised at Harris for the edge of cruelty in his tone. But Harris was away, fetching clean water.

I could at least make myself presentable for his return. My uniform was disgracefully spattered. One privilege of my position is that no officer will flog me for disorderly kit. Unlike poor McDowell, so terrified of a few spots of ash he made them his last words.

It disturbed me, Sheppard's story. That whole week, it had haunted me. Not for the outlandish content, but his conviction. Sheppard was afraid – so afraid that manly bluster was eclipsed entirely. I was accustomed to such unpleasantness in the operating theatre: a physiological reaction to a physical threat. But what was the root of Sheppard's terror? The spark that created this 'fireman' of his?

I tried to picture such a man. A ghoul who laughs and threatens to – what? In Sheppard's dreams, he invades a quiet Cromer parlour and opens his mouth. To bite, I wondered? Or to curse?

It were as if I had called for him. In the infirmary doorway, Sheppard had a jug of steaming water and a weary smile on his face. I experienced a queer feeling, as if someone had shone a light on my inner-most thoughts. In a trice, I was sickened, outraged – and, I realised, prickling with fear. As Sheppard stood there, brazenly scrutinising me with bloodshot eyes, I considered how easy it would be to snatch up any one of my surgical implements and extinguish him like a lamp.

What a fool I had been.

'Where is Harris?' I demanded.

A smear of ash marred the stoker's slackened mouth.

He would not tell.

With an oath, I was on my feet. I broke my duty of care to the men lying around me. Sheppard made no attempt to stop me leaving. I moved as if through a dream, down ladders, slipping and bumping with the fevered motion of the waves. I passed the spot where Walsh met his end, where McDowell – talkative McDowell – had failed to die when Sheppard first pushed him.

No preternatural creature could com-pel a man to murder. I made this my litany as I raced to the engine room. Sails were up. Even deep in the bowels of the ship, I could hear them clinking urgently above the relentless churning of the boilers. At the engine room hatch I faltered, seized by the heat emanating from within. I should have brought a pistol. I was too soft for this, whatever it was. I ought to return to my post, to wait for Harris with a plate of buttered bread and some hot tea to toast his return. Oh, but how then to live with myself? With my hands on the iron wheel, I set my teeth against the burn, my eyes shut tight against whatever lay inside.

I could call his name,
yet I could not.

Everyone would
know.

OASIS

by Anna Ojinnaka
Illustration by Zuzanna Kwiecien

My wife and I lived in the desert, *in a house of my own design. It was a structure of glass and steel, open and spacious, just like the terrain. When the sun set on the horizon and the stars came out to play, it would feel like we were living in our very own planetarium.*

We were both lovers of the desert, of the outlandish views it gifted us. It was a world of extremes where there was nothing and nowhere to hide. If not for our house, our little oasis, then we would die from exposure either day or night. Nothing was done in half measures in such a harsh place, but to us that felt something like the truth, of honesty. What we saw was what we got, and there were few things in life that we could say the same about.

My wife respected how dangerous the desert could be. Her car would always be stocked with water even if she was just driving into town. She knew what to do in an emergency and had a great sense of direction, so when she didn't return home one day, I called the authorities immediately. I felt numb when they declared her a missing person after sending a search team into the desert. They'd found her car, but not much else. She had seemingly disappeared without a trace. Her family and friends were devastated, and I knew what they were all thinking: they all thought she was dead. Deep down I thought it too, but I wasn't ready to accept that she was gone, not until her body was found. I was in denial, of course. It was hard to imagine anyone lasting days in the desert with limited water, no food, and full exposure. Still, I waited for her to return. It was a stupid, almost whimsical thing to do, but I kept the front door unlocked in case she found her way back home.

Nine days later, and that's exactly what happened. It was the middle of the day and I was drifting off in my study when I heard the front door open and then shut with a bang, jolting me out of my reverie. I rushed downstairs immediately, praying that I hadn't inevitably allowed an intruder to walk into my home, when I saw her, my wife, standing at the base of the stairs with a dazed expression on her face. Her clothes were dusty and her long brown hair was dishevelled, but otherwise she looked to be in good shape; there was not a scratch on her body. What concerned me was the way she was looking up at me, as if she was struggling to remember who I was. For a minute, I panicked, the possibility of amnesia entering my mind, but then she spoke my name. It was more of a question than anything else, her tone rising at the last syllable, but it was sweet relief. I hurried down the stairs and took her in my arms. My tears touched her neck and her shoulders and when she hugged me back, her arms squeezing me tightly, I knew that she was real.

'Lindsey...' I uttered. It was good to be able to say her name again.

The next few days were a whirlwind. I'd told everyone that she had returned in one piece, and they were just as ecstatic as I was. It felt like a miracle. We had a lot of visitors. Most people came simply to share their joy at having her back, to see and to hold Lindsey in their arms when they thought they never would again.

We had a visit from the local police, who simply wanted a statement from Lindsey about the events of her disappearance, but she was very vague. She rubbed her temples and shook her head, claiming that her time in the desert was a blur and that she'd rather forget the experience altogether. The police were understanding and didn't probe for more details. Neither did I. I wanted to give Lindsey all the time and space she needed to heal after her traumatic experience, so I didn't question her changed demeanor or her lapses in memory. She had to ask me where the bathroom was and where things were kept, but I didn't want to subject her to an interrogation. Like everyone else, I was just happy to have her back.

I did start to worry when all her former interests seemed to fall by the wayside. Since she had come back, her only interest seemed to be eating. I was sympathetic, as I knew that it was a common way for people to relieve stress, but it really took me by surprise when she, a strict vegetarian, took it upon herself to make us a steak dinner. I had come from work when I smelled the rich aroma of sizzling meat. She told me to get changed quickly so that we could sit down for dinner. That was another change; Lindsey never used to cook. The height of her culinary skills was microwaving a frozen meal.

When I sat down at the dinner table as instructed, I noticed that while she had cooked my steak well done, hers was not only rare, but still freely bleeding. I doubted if it had even touched the frying pan. It looked like it would go 'moo' if you poked it.

'This is new,' I said.

'What is?' she asked, cocking her head to the side. The movement was strangely reptilian. I quickly put the thought out of my mind.

'You eating meat. You haven't had a steak since you were about twelve.'

'Well, what can I say, Eric? Being out in the desert made me realise how much

I miss the taste of meat. You wouldn't believe the things I had to eat out there. Lizards, tarantulas, itty bitty things that barely filled my stomach. Nothing like this masterpiece.'

That was the first solid bit of information Lindsey had shared with me about her time in the desert. It was an awful thing to learn, but I was glad that Lindsey was finally opening up to me. I took the opportunity to learn more.

'Lindsey, can you remember what made you stop in the desert?'

Her eyes widened. 'What do you mean?'

I chose my next words carefully. 'The police said the car hadn't broken down. Did something make you stop?'

Lindsey shook her head. 'Can we talk about something else? Something that *won't* give me indigestion.'

She began to eat like her life depended on it, wolfing down every morsel without chewing. I stared, transfixed, as she even ate the T-bone. She caught me staring and grinned at me, her teeth stained red with blood.

It wasn't just her appetite for food that had increased, but also her appetite for sex. For this reason alone, it should not have come as a surprise to me when she revealed, before washing down her meal with a swig of wine, that she was pregnant. I almost choked on my dinner. We had wanted to start a family, yes, but I had assumed that after her awful ordeal she would want to put kids on hold until she was feeling more like herself again. It turns out I was completely wrong. She was beaming from ear to ear.

I tried to return her smile, as I did not want her to think that I was unhappy with the news, but the truth was that I didn't know what to think. I should've been happy, but all I felt was confusion, and, even worse, apprehension. My wife had changed since she'd come back and I was no longer sure if her time in the desert was entirely to blame. There were times when

I felt like I was living with someone who only looked like my wife, an impostor. I didn't want to dwell on such a ridiculous notion, so I focused on Lindsey's pregnancy instead.

Lindsey's stomach ballooned practically overnight. On the third day after she'd told me of her pregnancy, she looked like she was ready to go into labour. I insisted, practically begged, that she see a doctor. I was no obstetrician, but I knew that her belly growing to the size of a watermelon in three days, rather than three trimesters, was a cause for concern. Lindsey, however, was adamant that she was fine and that she didn't need to see anyone.

'Every pregnancy is different,' she said to me, but what was even more disturbing than her inflated stomach were her cravings. I caught her on the sofa, watching a cooking program on our widescreen TV, while snacking on a bowl of meat. Raw meat.

'I'm eating for two now,' she explained when she saw me staring, and she popped another red cube into her mouth. 'Speaking of which, can you go into town to get some more beef? Not the cheap kind like these watery cubes--I want premium cuts.'

I decided that enough was enough. I had tried to understand Lindsey's odd behaviour. I had tried to give her space and not to judge, but something was clearly wrong and she needed to see a doctor. I walked over to where she was sitting and snatched the bowl right out of her hands. She gasped as if I'd just torn her first born child away from her.

'Lindsey, I'm taking you to a doctor. Now.'

Lindsey scoffed. She folded her arms and leaned back into the couch. 'You can try.'

I reached out to place a hand on her shoulder. It was meant to be a reassuring touch. I wanted her to know that I was on her side, that I was only thinking of her safety as well as the baby's, but she didn't see it that way at all.

'I'm not going!' She shrieked. I saw the flash of sharp, bone-white teeth.

I cried out in pain. Lindsey bit me. She actually bit me. I withdrew my hand and backed away. I looked in horror at the damage her teeth had caused. It was not the bite mark of a human being. There were deep punctures in the flesh. I staggered back and stumbled over the coffee table, ending up on the hardwood floor. Lindsey stood up from her seat, her eyes wide, and she began to apologise profusely.

'Oh, my god. I'm so sorry, Eric. I didn't mean to.'

Before she came any closer to me, I put up my good hand and told her to back off. I hadn't imagined what I'd seen. My injured hand was proof of that.

I got to my feet and ran out of the house as fast as my legs would take me. At that point, I was running for my life. I got into my car and sped away. From the rearview mirror, I could see Lindsey standing by the front door. Tears glistened in her eyes while blood shone on her lips like gloss.

***

I ended up in my office. I needed to calm down so that I could make sense of what was going on, and there was no better place. I still had some blueprints on my desk, each building design painstakingly rendered from careful measurements. I had to be just as precise assessing my current situation. What did I see, exactly? I saw Lindsey's face transform into something monstrous. Her teeth had looked like needles and her eyes had looked like those of a snake, but it had only been for a second, when she bit into my hand. Could I have imagined such a thing? I looked at my injured hand. The wound throbbed in time to the beating of my heart. I had treated it using the supplies in the first-aid cabinet, but I'd have to seek medical attention at some point to be safe. The last thing I wanted was an infection.

My phone buzzed in my pocket and I pulled it out quickly. It was Lindsey. My heart hammered unpleasantly in my chest. I hit the call button and brought the phone up to my ear.

'Lindsey?' I said shakily.

Lindsey sniffed. 'I'm sorry, Eric. I really did try, but I see now that I can't be your wife... or a mother to our child.'

I shot up from my seat. 'Lindsey, what the hell are you talking about? Listen, I'm sorry for running away. I shouldn't have left you all alone. I'm on my way back right now.'

'Promise me that you'll take care of the child.'

'What? Of course I'm going to take of our child—'

The line went dead. I ran out of the office and made my way back home immediately.

The first thing that caught my attention when I reached the house was the open front door. Red liquid was caked onto the handle, and I hoped that it wasn't what I thought it was. I got out of the car and moved towards the front door, feeling even more tense when I noticed that there were bloody footprints leading out of it. They got fainter until finally they disappeared completely into the desert. I was about to take my phone out to call the police, but then I heard it. The sound of a baby crying. It sounded alarmingly loud in the silence of the desert at dusk. I burst through the front door and ran up the stairs, two at a time, until I reached the room where the sound was coming from. It was our room, mine and Lindsey's. I opened the door and there it was, a newborn baby, still covered in afterbirth, laying on the centre of our bed. The white sheets were soaked in blood and I could see where the footprints outside had originated from: a sticky red puddle on the pinewood floor. The room looked like a murder scene. I had to take a moment to steady myself, to anchor myself back to reality.

The baby was red in the face from crying. I walked over to the wardrobe, avoiding the sticky footprints on the floor, and pulled out a fresh towel from the drawer. I used it to gently wipe the blood off the baby's – my baby's – face. I took it into my arms and held it close. It looked like a perfectly normal, healthy baby—except for the fact that it already had a full set of teeth. Unable to find anything to pacify it with, I put the tip of my index finger into its mouth. As soon as it latched onto the digit, its little milk teeth bit into the flesh. I let out a cry of pain and pulled my finger back. To my horror, I watched as the baby's tongue lolled out of its mouth, savouring the blood it had drawn from my finger, its unseeing eyes gazing up at me blindly. When it was finished, its face screwed up and it began to cry once more. I winced at the sound, which was even more excruciating with the baby right next to my chest.

I placed my bleeding finger back into its mouth, and just as I'd predicted, it

began to calm down. I didn't bother calling out for Lindsey. I knew that she was never coming back again. It would be terrible, having to explain to Lindsey's family that she was gone once more, but the truth is that I don't think it was really her who came back in the first place. Who, or what, I had shared a child with was a mystery to me, but I would keep my promise. I would look after the child, even if it did possess its mother's monstrous cravings. I'd have to find a new place for us to live because the desert was no longer a place I could call home. I had been made privy to its secrets, and I, once welcoming of the truth, wished for those secrets to be buried, just as surely as my wife was buried somewhere beneath the sands.

BLACK SLAB

by Ashley Stokes

Nigel says you mustn't touch it, *so you do touch it. The new wardrobe door is warm. Moist and kind of sweaty, it reminds you of Nigel's back if he's been in a sauna. A sensation spreads from your fingertips to your palm. The veins in your wrist tingle. The door doesn't want you to touch it. You whip your hand away.*

You don't know how a six-foot high, black wardrobe in a monumental, headstone-like style was delivered and assembled without waking you. You don't know how Nigel has managed to break up the old wardrobe without disturbing you. Speckled with dust and wood chips, your clothes and his are all over the floor. The new wardrobe is so black it seems to suck the light from the room.

Nigel is wearing trackie bottoms, nothing else. He is fat from months of pizza and booze. He looks like shit. You look like shit. You have both been indoors for three months. The bedroom smells musty. You long to open the window, let in some air. You don't trust air. No one trusts air anymore.

A pulse squirms behind your right eye. Last night's Merlot. You used to have a T-shirt with 'You had me at Merlot' printed on it. You used to sleep in your own bed, too, and your husband used to be sane. Last night, after dusk fell, your husband forced you from room to room. She was following you, he said repeatedly. She was back. She wants you. She can't have you. Finally, you cracked open the wine to shut him out.

You slept on the sofa. Nigel passed out in the armchair.

You don't remember him leaving the room this morning. You remember the dream that woke you again, two of him in fancy dress staring at you. Then you had tramped upstairs to find this black monstrosity dominating the bedroom.

'Don't touch it,' says Nigel. 'As Mr Gill, my old woodwork teacher would say, wood needs to breathe.'

Nigel steps in front of you, as if shielding you from the black thing. You want to ask him why he ordered a wardrobe you don't need. You want to ask him how we can afford it, tell him how upset you are.

You no longer expect him to make sense, though. He may have been outside. He may have breathed it in.

Nigel's other things are packed in a rucksack: the final map, the torch, the crowbar. When you step back, you notice the book poking out from a side-pocket of the rucksack.

You slink sideways. Keeping an eye on him, in case he turns around, you pluck out the book and hide it behind your back.

You shudder. 'I'm going to be sick, Nige.'

***

In the kitchen, you hide the book in the knife drawer. You drink a pint of water and, relieved you have not tempted fate, keep it down. Through the patio doors, you can't help hating the degree to which the grass needs cutting. The borders sprawl. The leylandii hedge is bushy and looms. How you would like to go out there and make a start: the snip of secateurs, the crisp click of shears, the whirr of the mower. It is illegal to go outside unless you have a role essential to the skeleton economy. You have already been fined a thousand pounds when a drone caught you parked at the trig point at Ditching Heights to get away from Nigel for an hour. You have been fined £1000, and Nigel still orders a wardrobe that you don't need.

Nigel has breathed in the spores. Must have.

You remember filling up at Bruton's Garage when you were still giving lessons during The Scare, still an instructor for the Arpeggio Driving School, and old Bruton came out and stood next to you as you stuck the nozzle into the petrol cap. He pointed at the woods over at Nether Mundham. He sounded grizzled. He said, 'they've always lurked there, now they've come out.'

He must have been one of the first around here to have breathed them in and started to see things before he vanished. A few weeks later Kelly from the office texted that Mrs Cope's boy, Kalvin, had vanished. The weird kid you taught to drive once upon a time. Nigel's old teacher Mr Gill had vanished, too. The new landlord of the Swan with Two Necks that Kelly had been trying to get her hooks into was not returning her texts. He's married. She's married. She should have known better. The last you heard of Kelly, though, she said she'd seen The Anaesthetist on her driveway, lit up in her burglar lights. Next, she saw him in her kitchen and later at the end of her bed with his mask and some sort of black stick. That freak was from the sixties and whoever committed those crimes back then must now be dead. An imposter? A copycat? Kelly hallucinating? They say that if you breathe in the spores you see things, hear things.

Outside, the grass ripples like it wants to stroke you. The hedge spreads like it wants to strap you in to the recesses the breezes open and close. You remember other times when Nigel would be cutting the hedge and you would bring him a beer. You remember when Quarantine was announced. You thought this might bring you and Nigel close again. You might talk now, about Ella, the one that got so far you gave her a name. You might desire him again, and he you. You might spend all this endless time stuck inside together trying to salvage something before it's too late.

You try to pinpoint the exact moment you realised that this was not going to happen. You would not melt into him and he melt into you as if it were a long time ago again.

At first you had put Nigel's behaviour down to him still grieving Ella in some selfish way that excluded you and your grief and made it all about him. You know you used this to explain to yourself why he was pretending to his drinking mates in The Quiet Woman that he was shagging Tarsh from Design and the temp in Accounts they called JoJo Binks. Kelly's husband Blobby Craig had told Kelly that, and she told you, but when you had it out with Nigel you did believe him that he was trying to make himself more interesting than just the middle-aged data goon to his hipster-twat colleagues at Celerie Blu and Kelly's fat husband.

You did not believe that all was otherwise well with Nigel, though, and that was before The Scare, Quarantine and what everyone was now calling The Great Disorder.

Quite early on you suspected that Nigel was sneaking outside. That faraway, distracted look and slight drawl to his speech now was because he'd breathed in the spores. He'd probably crept out to smoke when he was supposed to have given up, or he'd sloped into the garden to text other women when he'd sworn blind his conquests were the beer talking. It could have been simple stir-craziness, or just because, stuck indoors with you all day, you do his head in.

The first time you remember thinking something was really up was when he read a book. You don't know where the book came from. He said he'd found it in a box in the garage that contained that stack of old *PC User* magazines he'd bought at a car boot for some geeky reason. You'd never seen him read a book before, not a story book, fiction, make-believe. Biographies of golfers, footballers and eighties tech pioneers, yes. Textbooks when he was taking his MBA, yes. Updated data protection regulations, yes. Never shown a flicker of interest in much else. When he found that book, the book you have hidden in the knife drawer for later, he sat with it for three days, read it through God knows how many times.

When he set it aside, he told you he'd seen a statue of 'a moose-headed thing' in the garden. That was on the same day he started to make the maps.

On sheets of thin, grey paper so vast they flopped over the kitchen table, Nigel worked on architectural drawings of the layout of the house. First the downstairs, the kitchen, lounge, breakfast-diner and hallway, over and over until all was in proportion and perfect, no smudges, no wonky lines. This process was repeated for the upstairs, the bedroom, bathroom, guest-bedroom-cum-office and the landing. When this diagram had been versioned and reversioned until it could sit exactly on top of the first drawing, he started to add to it a coiling maze of narrow tunnels that connected a network of regular and irregular-shaped chambers.

Something about it reminded you of

intestines.

The house now had guts.

Guts on the outside.

When the maps of the tunnels fitted onto one sheet of Nigel's vast paper, he started to clip other sheets to the drawing. A huge expanse was suggested, a desert that surrounded the house: dunes, ruins, mountains and crevasses, all drawn in violet pencil strokes distinct from the uniform black of the house and tunnels.

You did ask him what it was.

'The Vex Prismatic,' he said.

'The what?'

You noticed the book. It was on the table, almost entirely covering your bedroom: the heart of the whole map.

You picked it up. You had always disliked the cover. You opened it to the contents page. The titles of the stories gave you the creeps. He snatched the book from you.

'Don't,' he said. 'She'll know.'

'Who, Nigel?'

'The Compiler.'

***

Outside, the breeze eddies in the long grass. Your breath mists the glass of the patio door. Outside seems foggy. You wonder if you should go outside and breathe in the fog. You could join Nigel then, see what he sees. You could be together. When this ends, when the spores dissipate or the authorities find a way to fumigate or inoculate, you don't know if he will recover, if you will be the same, if you can still let him be your last chance, or if you should melt into one mad thing. You wonder if this is what the dream you have each morning means, the dream that two Nigels are watching you, both in sheets made from filthy scraps of sacking and rags, both with gaping black Halloween-costume eyes.

An outline is reflected in the glass, haloes the rainbow edges of the mist patch.

Someone stands behind you.

You turn.

No one there.

A thud-thud-thud down the stairs.

Nigel, still topless and sockless, stomps into the room, then freezes, head swaying like a cat's when you think it can see someone you can't.

'We need to move,' you say. 'We need to leave this house. Too much …'

'Don't move,' he says, and circles around you, arm raised.

'You need to see someone, Nigel.'

'Can't you see her?'

'I can no longer see her. Can you still see her?'

He stands in front of you. He clenches his fists at his sides. His love handles bulge and ripple. He stares at the doorway. He stalks towards it, that low, hunched walk you remembered from when you went paintballing that time with the Celerie Blu team.

You follow him up the stairs.

He is paused on the landing. You can see the black slab in the bedroom over his shoulder. He appears to have dragged it across the room. You don't remember hearing him do this while you were at the patio door.

'It's you she wants,' he says.

'There's no one here.'

'In the violet dress. There! There!'

He points at nothing.

There is nothing between the pair of you and the black slab.

He is telling some story to himself.

He is its hero.

It is horrible to see.

If you report their distress, they are collected. Some threads say they vanish into some sort of red-tape nightmare. Some that, if you leave them to let it work its way out, they vanish anyway, like Kalvin vanished, and Mr Bruton and Mr Gill vanished. Some part of Nigel has already vanished.

It's too much for you, this realisation. You leave him, creep backwards downstairs.

***

You take the book from the knife drawer. It is fragile and thin, its spine loose and its jacket distressed. *The Underkin and Other Stories* by Astrea Themis. You hate the cover. Frozen sludge seen from above, scum smeared across a fly's eye, a skein of scratchy, scribbly typographic gestures that floats in the last glimmerings of the last dusk. Something like that.

You tease open the book.

The contents page jumps out at you.

You were sure that the middle run of stories was:

Orange Slab
Men Shall Know Nothing of This
Fields and Scatter
Cretaceous

Now it's:

Orange Slab
Men Shall Know Nothing of This
Black Slab
Fields and Scatter
Cretaceous

You turn and look over your shoulder.

No one stands in the doorway between this room and the room beyond.

You call his name.
You call him to you.
You turn to the page.
Black Slab

You will soon wish that you still have friends who could explain that what is written in **Black Slab** is a coincidence. It's a random quirk that a writer in 1961 could write a story that describes the haunting of you as Nigel experienced it; that so many stories are written by so many writers that one must unintentionally become predictive to someone somewhere; or that **Black Slab** is some elaborate hoax of Nigel's; or an account of Nigel's madness, Nigel reaching out to you, confiding the vividness of his disordered mind.

You will wish that someone you used to know could help you decipher this. You will wish that someone could explain to you how Astrea Themis sixty years ago could write a story called **Black Slab** in which a man called Nigel and a woman called Hayley are trapped together in their house during a bizarre and unprecedented invasion of cosmic spores that have lain dormant under the woods at Nether Mundham for thousands of years and cause our deepest darkest fears to manifest and consume us. Early in the story, Nigel reads a story called **Black Slab** in a book called *The Underkin and Other Stories* by Astrea Themis in which a man called Nigel pursues a ghost that haunts his wife to a place from which he cannot return. As soon as he's completed the story, he is tempted outside by a representation of the fiend Lempo who whispers that an apparition called The Compiler wants to feed from what's inside Hayley. The Compiler appears to Nigel as an upright violet shimmer that looms over his wife when she's near corners or passageways in their house. He chases it from room to room. When The Compiler springs an interdimensional portal hidden in a black wardrobe on Nigel, he chases her back through it, into a maze of tunnels and caves, rooms beyond rooms, temples beneath temples, and then to the Vex Prismatic, a world of violet skies, violet dunes and ruins over which a three-pointed star hangs and into which The Compiler fades and loses him. The final lines of the story describe Nigel atop some landscape feature called The Great Roof, looking out over a sprawling, collapsed structure. The last sentence is obscure, more baffling than any other: 'So calmly greens the Temple of the Lonely One.'

***

You will soon wish you had not scrambled upstairs as soon as you finished the last page of the story, that you had fled into whatever lives in the air outside. You will wish that you had not found yourself rounding and rounding the black wardrobe that's now shrunken, shrinking, freezing, sealed and doorless. You will wish that you had not uttered *Nigel, Nigel, Nigel* a hundred times, that you had not been distracted by how many Nigels there were if Nigel had believed he was the Nigel in the story who believed he was the Nigel in the story who believed he was the Nigel in the story that Nigel was reading. You will wish you had realised earlier that I was behind you, following in my violet dress and my book and my inks ready. You will wish that you felt me shadowing you earlier, our circuits spiralling, closing, tightening as the black slab shrivels. You wish you are not now alone with me and mine, the two of them and their tatters, the fiend and its lusts. You whisper my name and I whisper yours. I come close, my eyes reflected in your eyes, a violet swarm in your fathomless pupils. I read you your last page for the first time.

THE HEAVIEST BURDEN

by Mike Adamson

*L**en Blake had never been slow to accept a dare, along with the reality that sometimes things went wrong. But tonight, as he crouched in the chill darkness, he admitted to himself he may have been overreaching this time.*

Hard times bred hard people, and things were difficult in modern Britain. No one was really surprised if you saw a big score and went after it, and Len had done his share of break-ins in the past few years. Carefully scoped-out targets, of course, always when the occupants were away, and nothing too fancy on the security: no dogs, no close neighbours, no house-sitters. Easy-peasy, most of the time, just like this job had seemed when Freddie had talked him into it.

Freddie was the one who disposed of stolen goods, and did the paying out, and he had a cherry job lined up for any mug who'd take it. Len now winced as he realised he was the mug in question. But he had never before been guaranteed a thousand pounds, cash in hand, for a single item. He could go straight for a while on that—wash cars, wash windows, something that didn't carry a jail term if caught.

That was all very well, but now he was facing the job, something about it was off-putting. In fact if he'd felt this way before, he'd have told Freddie to keep looking.

Len huddled in his heavy jacket, wool hat down against the night wind that droned across rank grass outside the tall wire fences of the Northern Air Museum, a few miles in from the Durham coast. A few spotlights glared through the dark, picked out the corners of the admin building and hangars, and silhouetted the outdoor exhibits—a Bloodhound missile on its launcher, a Vulcan bomber, long overdue for restoration, both relics of the Cold War...

He had visited the museum a couple of days ago on a mild autumn afternoon, to look over the job, and had wondered if his imagination was running away with him. He was the only visitor on a quiet weekday, and the airy hangars, the storage sheds filled with vintage aircraft and the parts thereof, had seemed...dead. Cold, so terribly cold, as if ice might form at any moment. He had never felt so chilled to the bone before, and had been glad to leave, get back into the weak sun and breathe air free of the scents of oil and decayed antiquity.

He had seen the object in question, of course, in the World War II hangar. A document in a glass frame: a yellowed, heavy-stock letter in German, with an Alte Deutsche script heading and the eagle of the Third Reich. What made it valuable was the signature at the foot—Adolf Hitler. It was an operational order rerouting bombers to a high-priority target, but at the Fuhrer's personal command. In and of itself, it was a piece of paper, eighty-years old, which had been touched by a lunatic, and it was well known among historians and aviation buffs. But to a black market collector, it was worth a small fortune, and Freddie had a buyer lined up. All he needed was someone to do the business, and Len, foolishly, had put his hand up for it.

The museum was out in the country, a long-disused RAF station. He heard the distant drone from a motorway in a cutting at the end of a pot-holed lane, but otherwise he was alone but for owls and mice. Clouds hid the stars, and the night wind sighed in skeletal trees, their leaves now a crackling carpet. Halloween had come and gone, and the country was on its long slide toward snow; things were at a low ebb in nature, as well as among human doings in depressed and desperate times.

Which brought him back to that thousand pounds, and what he could do with it—take Jan for a week in Whitby, maybe, now the cheap season was in—yet, also, how uncomfortable he was with the job. Not that it was beyond him, it should have been a doddle; he'd scoped out the entry pathway, and the place had squat-all decent security, not even a dog loose after hours. But there were stories about why that might be. Oh, yes, there were stories, he had heard them over brown ale in pubs. The sort of stories he laughed at, but, now he was here, alone in the dark, he had to wonder.

Strange sounds. Lights in the hangars when it was known no one was about, and *not* the main lights set on timer to illuminate at random... Voices. Things out of place, rearranged night after night. Even those who whispered of it in the close air of back bars did not want to say too much, and a strange aura of the sinister had settled upon the museum. Len scoffed at such things in the light of day, as a decent burglar he knew there was nothing in the dark that wasn't there in the light, and he had taken the job with the feeling of earning easy money.

Freddie was expecting a result, and did not like being disappointed. He could have a nasty side, and Len had no wish to provoke it. So he brought wire clippers from a coat pocket and ran doubled through the long grass to the foot of the chain-link fence, out of sight of roads and squarely behind the dark bulk of a hangar. The wire cut with reassuring simplicity and he opened a gap next to a post, drew the rattling mass aside and squeezed through.

To a pro with even a little experience, the owners could not have made it easier. He crossed to the corner of the hangar, stayed low and kept watch. Nothing moved and he knew there were no motion sensors. The museum had only old-fashioned alarms wired to doors and windows, he had seen them on his reconnaissance visit, and Freddie had managed a look at the plans due to some nefarious contact in the local council.

The World War II display was the next hangar over, a sprawling place adjoining the administration building. He ran in a crouch from a pile of building materials to the gutted remnants of a Navy helicopter, paused to watch and listen, then sprinted across a patch of worn concrete to the disembodied forward fuselage of a Hawker Hunter jet fighter awaiting restoration. From there it was just a breathless ten-second race to the black shadows by the foot of the metal wall, dimly-lit in the spill from a lonely spotlight picking out the doors to the admin building.

Len's heart was racing. It was usually up there on a job, adrenaline helped keep him sharp, and fear was natural. But something beyond caution was whispering at the back of his mind, though he could not put his finger on it.

He shuffled along the base of the wall to a stack of materials, rotting wooden pallets from deliveries long ago, and knew he was well up to his own schedule as he heaved a crate onto the stack, mounded up several planks on top of that, and had a virtual stairway. He ran up it, took easy hold of the guttering and hoisted onto the corrugated steel roof. The sheeting ran up at a steep angle to join a curved roof section over the tallest point of the hangar, on its midline. In a short vertical wall segment below the curved roof were the windows of bathrooms on a mezzanine level, and he swarmed up the steel sheet roof to the grimy window he knew served the upstairs men's washroom.

Now he was on his own turf he smiled smugly as he used a rotary diamond cutter to take a piece out of the window, reached in and disconnected the alarm circuit with a quick snip, then freed off the old window latch. He drew out the angled pane, fed himself through and, with the greatest care, lowered himself to the floor beside the sinks.

There were no locks on the bathroom doors and he was out into the museum in moments. The document was in a display of World War II memorabilia, artefacts from the war years, on the far side of the hangar, and he flicked a small LED penlight to life to make his way down creaking metal stairs.

And as he reached the bottom, he froze, for he was sure he heard a voice.

Just a murmur in the gloom...the hangar was crowded with restored aircraft, and dim nightlights created jagged silhouettes, a feeling of being in a metal jungle. He snapped off his penlight and crouched, waited, listening intently, but the whisper was gone, and he replayed the sound in his head over and over. If someone was working late, there should be more sign, a batch of the overhead neon tubes on somewhere, a radio playing, something...

God, it was cold... Len shivered as he realised the chill seemed to be striking up at him from the concrete floor, that same dread cold he had felt on his last visit. He breathed steam and flicked his penlight on again, to send the beam cautiously about. The propeller blades of a fibreglass replica Spitfire gleamed close by, and he crept past it to the rotten remains of an unrestored German Bf 109, missing its wings. Just beyond, an original American jeep waited under the wing of a Westland Lysander, posed in a life-size recreation of a spy mission departing for occupied Europe.

All this was very interesting on one level, but the frozen tableau of a bygone age was just a little creepy, too, Len thought.

Preserving memories of the war years had become a passion and industry for thousands, but many today were disturbed by thoughts of that vast global conflagration. All that death... And the decorations, minus the light of day, held their own macabre edge, for shop mannequins, dressed in period garb, standing in for the players in the scene, seemed surreal in the gloom, as if they would jerk to plastic life if one glanced away.

Len whirled as he heard the voice again, and this time the distinct ring as a tool fell.

Heart in his mouth, he flattened out on the floor, but the cold was more than he could bear, forcing him up on trembling limbs after a few moments. He was definitely not alone in here, but he could not see who was there, nor was there any direction to the sounds.

Sense told him to turn and get out the way he came in, before he was spotted. If he was arrested, he would be doing three months, at least, and keeping his mouth shut on Freddie's behalf, if he knew what was good for him. He could do without that. Yet he was but twenty metres from the prize now, and saw the memorabilia display in dimmed spotlights.

It filled a room constructed from steel mesh, a gigantic cage, in which were all manner of Forties things—gas masks and ration books, propaganda posters and newspapers, uniforms in display cases, all lovingly preserved under glass. Len concentrated on the job, moved with one stealthy step after another, eased by a display of disarmed ordnance, bombs, rockets, even an aerial torpedo, and reached the door of the cage. It stood open in daytime, but, due to the value of the relics within, was closed after hours with a bright, new padlock.

With a last look around for whomever was working here, Len reached into his deep coat pockets and brought out the tool for the job. Bolt-cutters were a precision item, and he screwed long handles into place by touch alone, the light off but still held in his teeth.

He could see glimmers on the glass of the framed Hitler document, just a few metres away, all he need do was open the door, take down the frame, slit the backing paper and remove the document. It would roll into a plastic tube in his pocket, and he would be out and free in three minutes.

But as he put the bolt cutters to the padlock, he heard a soft cough, and his head snapped around.

Light...

Blue-edged light was shining faintly from the troop windows of the biggest plane in the hangar, an old American Dakota—a standard twin-engine transport plane of the war. The type had delivered tens of thousands of paratroops and incalculable quantities of cargo, towed gliders and extracted wounded, a maid of all work, synonymous with victory. The windows of this one shone softly with a bluish glow, and Len froze for long moments.

Who..? He smiled faintly. It could just be kids, trespassing, locked in after hours, they had found a hidey-hole to drink, maybe shag... They would be in dead trouble if they were not out before morning. But, as he relaxed for a moment, Len asked himself the obvious next question—how did they get in?

Then he heard the music. Just a faint whisper, as if a radio were playing very softly—but it was *swing*, Forties big band, the very sound of the era. And for no reason he could imagine, cold sweat broke at his brow, and he felt faint... He no longer had the strength to cut the padlock loop, and let the cutters go down. He panted softly, stared longingly at the paper he was sent to get, and glanced again at the Dakota. The light had intensified and the music was louder—not much, but definitely...louder.

Len gripped the bolt cutters in both hands like a weapon, took a shaky step toward the plane, and froze again as he heard laughter. A man's laugh, derisive, caustic in the things it masked, a sound of pain. It came softly through the chill gloom, and Len wondered what might be taking place in that old fuselage. Something awful, something a decent man, thief or no, should do something about? He was no featherweight when it came to a scrap, had done some damage in his days, and now he advanced, penlight in his pocket, making his way by the blue glow alone. He rounded the towering tail of the Dakota, to find the access door to the left, and the blue light spilled around the partly-open hatch with icy intensity.

The music jangled on, an anachronistic background, as Len saw his breath cloud the air, the blue glow shining through it. The cold was wicked now, he would have sworn frost was forming on the aircraft. His steps seemed loud in his ears, and he jerked painfully as he heard the grind of a boot sole on concrete somewhere to his left. He dropped into a crouch, stared into the shadows, but again, there was no one there. The laugh came once more, and he heard movement in the plane, but the light did not vary, remaining just that cold, blue aura...

Get out.

He did not know if the words were his own, as his better sense screamed at him, or if they were whispered to his mind from somewhere else. But they locked him in place for terrible moments, as his heart raced wildly. He should go, face Freddie's wrath, anything to be away from this! Yet he did not believe in things beyond the pale, and expected to find nothing more than a couple of teens with sleeping bags, dossing down with a radio and the kind of liquid anaesthetic that made life bearable. Anything else was his imagination: he told himself this firmly, stepped forward, and put out a hand to push the partly open door inward on its hinges, to reveal the interior.

He could not have said if it was a shock of static electricity that struck through his gloves, or simply the awful cold of the grave that seemed to flood from the aircraft, up his arm and close about his mind, but with the suddenness of a stroke of lightning he was no longer aware of his body, of his location, and saw as if through the eyes of

another. He was left breathless, for this was a window onto a lost reality in a way the museum only attempted to achieve.

The aircraft was trembling, the twin-radial engines brayed strong and clear, and the long body was packed with frightened men. Twenty-eight paratroopers, fourteen to each side of the aisle, had risen from the benches and waited in red light as orders were barked, and chute release lines were hooked onto the static line overhead as they readied. Somehow, Len knew this was D-Day, June 6th 1944, and these were among the first men to land in occupied Europe, in the hours before dawn, when the great seaborne force would roll in on the five target beaches.

A light over the exit door changed from red to green and the jumpmaster NCO began to count the men out. They stepped into the rushing darkness and vanished, one after another, going to their fate with stoic courage, lugging masses of gear, flinging themselves into space to defy the evil that held the world in thrall...

All but for the last man. Len could hardly make out his features, behind goggles, and decorated with black camouflage paint, but he seemed to be unable to take that last step. He jammed in the hatch and froze, and the jumpmaster roared for him to go. The pilot called back, demanding to know if he was clear to begin the pull away to safety, but the man could not move.

The sergeant needed to follow his men but the last was screaming now, his hands locked to the door frame, and nothing the sergeant could do could free them. He tried to shove the man out, but with every second they grew farther and farther from the rest of the unit. Bellowed words made no difference, and the terror gripping the last man was appalling to behold. And at last, Len understood the horror of the moment, for the sergeant drew his side arm, put it to the man's ribs and punched off two savage shots.

In the roar of engines and wind, the

reports were almost lost, and the body tumbled free, before the sergeant called the last away and jumped after his unit, leaving the cabin empty as the pilot began his pull away.

***

Len opened his eyes and found himself cold to the bone, slumped on the hard concrete under the aircraft's tail. The hangar was utterly silent and the blue light had gone. He massaged his nerveless hands as he fought to his knees, pulled out the penlight and looked around. The bolt cutters lay nearby and he grabbed them up, to rise and back away from the old plane.

What a terrible thing to happen... Now he understood. It was not the fear, not even the pain, nor the fact a life had been taken.

It was the shame.

Shame bound that tortured soul to the last place it had known in life, a shuddering, uncomfortable aircraft cabin, in the dark, amid terror and the thunder of engines and flak. Shame that he had not

been able to throw himself into that dread blackness with his comrades, land where he may and do battle, as part of the greatest invasion the world had ever known. Fear was understandable, an appreciation of how insane the events of that day had been, but to the individual, to have failed in the expectations of friends, family and society, was too much to bare.

And so he was bound forever to this piece of metal, seeking perhaps redemption, certainly unable to face those who had gone before him.

Now, when Len heard a voice, it was only sobbing he made out, edged with an inwardly-turned fury that seemed to threaten at any moment to erupt into poltergeist games, and Len Blake forgot all about parchments, Freddie and thousand pound rewards, to run with every ounce of strength he had for the stairs, the roof, and the clean countryside beyond.

HAVE A GHASTLY HALLOWEEN!

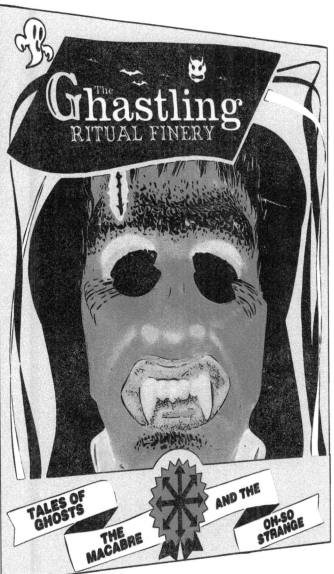

The Ghastling
RITUAL FINERY

THE FETCH
LARGE 12 TO 14
AS SEEN ON T.V.
35% COTTON FLANNEL 65% RAYON EXCLUSIVE OF ORNAMENTATION

© 2021 THE GHASTLING

TALES OF GHOSTS
THE MACABRE
AND THE
OH-SO STRANGE

'1.77

'1.77

GROW LIVE

MONSTERS GHOULS

myths of

MUMMIES

I FI

SPOOK-TACULAR

MORE MAD ROBOTS THIS ISSUE

MISTER MONSTER

RAVE

K

AAAAAAAAAGH

COFFIN CAPERS

THE MUMMY'S CURSE!

THE WERE WOLF OF LONDON

Night Creatures

CHAMBER of HORRORS GUILLOTINE

N

BARNABAS

HORROR MONSTERS

THEY

MASKS MASKS MASKS

MONSTER MAIL ORDER

MONSTER

ASTAROT

OF?

WEREWOLF

SURF

TERR

HORROR FILM CAVALCADE

MONSTER CRUSHERS!

BOO

YOUR OWN MONSTER FLY!

MAKING MONSTERS

RD

IG

PIRE?

OU AXED

DON'T BE A DROOP-OUT

METAL MONSTERS

FOR IT!

Dark

WEIRD VENGEA

shadows

RLEY

THE MAD

MONSTER FROM OUTER SPACE

GHOU

THE RAN-TAN MAN

by Simon John Parkin

I'd never heard of a ran-tan before the neighbours got together that day. It was the old guy from number 65 who stopped me when I was on my way back from work. 'Them buggers were up 'til all hours again last night,' he said as I passed him weeding his front garden in the sunshine one afternoon. 'Couldn't sleep they was making such a racket.' He wore the same heavy eyelids as me.

'Same here,' I said. 'I had work at eight this morning too'. We shook our heads and gave a malicious look towards the house in between where we lived, the downstairs window hanging out of its frame, a stained mattress and sodden doormat embedded in the nettles beneath a dilapidated 'To Let' sign.

'They keeping you up again, Bill?' the woman from over the road called from her front doorstep dressed in a flowery purple dressing gown. 'I told 'em to be quiet the other night but they just told me to eff off.'

'It's that bald one with the tattoos that causes all the trouble,' the old guy said, throwing his trowel into the soil. 'He was the one what broke in. Brings all his mates round, he does. As soon as they have a drop of drink all hell breaks loose.'

'Cars revving all night too,' the woman said.

'It's the music that gets me,' I joined in with the damnation, glad that I wasn't alone in my annoyance. 'It gets right through my ear plugs.'

The upstairs window of number 66 opened and a man in a vest top with a hot red face leaned out. 'You talking about him at 63?'

We all grumbled.

'I've tried phoning the police but they won't do anything,' he said. His muscular arm reached out and his finger jabbed downstairs. 'If those wasters wake my kids up on a school night I'm gonna go mental.'

Before long a group of us had formed: the fresh-faced couple who live at 62, the single mum from the other side of my house, a man I'd never seen before who came out of 67. All of us stood by the hedge outside the old guy's, discussing our errant neighbours. We moaned about the constant parties, the loud music, the shouting and fights that spilled out into the street. We cited the profanity that emanated from their broken windows and back-garden barbeques. We complained about the lost sleep, the loss of peace and restfulness in our own homes, the lack of control, the anxiety. It turned out that all of us had tried phoning either the police or the council but the police weren't interested and the council wanted months of carefully-logged evidence to back our claim.

The more we talked the louder we became in our condemnation, the weeks and weeks of frustration bubbling over. We all secretly hoped that they would overhear our vitriol.

'We should do something about them,' one of us whisper-shouted and we all agreed.

We plotted schemes for threatening them with eviction by a fake bailiff, barri-cading their door if they ever left for the day – anything to get them out. I could tell that these ideas had been concocted by over-tired, desperate minds in the middle of humid, noisy, sleepless nights. I didn't care though. My heart was racing at the thought of finally putting an end to the misery that was the bald git from next door.

I can't remember who suggested a ran-tan. It might have been the old guy, or maybe the bloke I'd never seen before from 67. Anyway, someone told us about how villages used to punish a person who violated community norms by banging pots and pans outside their house, sometimes for three days in a row, shaming them into leaving. It was almost like a parade, everyone getting together to oust the miscreant. They would make an effigy of them and drag it through the streets, pelting it with stones and setting it on fire.

'Sounds good to me,' I said. And the more we talked about it, as we raged at the soundly-sleeping neighbours, the more everyone thought it was the best way of dealing with them.

Before long, we had organised a date and apportioned tasks. The old guy was going to make flame torches, the woman from over the road would write a ran-tan song, the bloke who I'd never seen before was going to make a flyer to advertise it to any other disgruntled neighbours and I was to make an effigy.

***

It wasn't until I got back home that I began to wonder if maybe we were overreacting.

I felt shamefully petty as I started making the effigy, collecting old clothes to use from the bottom of my wardrobe. I found a tatty black and red t-shirt and a blazer that didn't fit any more which, together, looked similar to how the next-door neighbour dressed. I tied up the arms and half-heartedly stuffed them with scrunched-up newspaper. For the legs I got a pair of sweatpants and painted them with green slashes to look like the camo trousers that the neighbour perpetually wore. I stuffed the sweat pants too and tucked them into an old pair of Slazengers for his feet.

I sat the life-size figure up on the sofa – a headless bogeyman in my front room – and closed the curtains so that nobody could see. Even though I felt childish for making a Guy in my thirties my blood began to boil as I looked at the decapitated likeness of the man who had caused me so much grief over the last few months.

As I set about making his head from papier-mâché in the kitchen sink I thought about the months of torture I had endured.

It started with a rustle and clunk from outside my bedroom window one night. I didn't take any notice but it must have been him breaking in through the downstairs window. The house had been empty for a while, the landlords living in another country and leaving it in an un-rentable state. The next day there were echoing footsteps coming from next door and a scrawled sign on the door: 'Legal warning. Take notice: That we live in this property, it is our home and we intend to stay here. That at all times there is at least one person in this property. That if you want to get us out you will have to issue a claim in the County Court or in the High Court.'

That night was obviously his house-warming. People started turning up at 9. I could see him through my curtains in the front garden, grinning proudly as he welcomed his mates into the squatted house. The music – thudding, pounding music from speakers that somebody wheeled in – started up around 10 and was still going while I was trying to eat my breakfast the next morning, blearily getting ready for work, furious at my new neighbours. I had put ear plugs in but the bass cut right through them like it was hammering into my head. I had banged

on the wall but I don't think anyone heard me. I had phoned the police around 5am but they impatiently said that parties weren't against the law and that there wasn't much they could do. I gave up on sleep and watched crap morning telly until dawn, jumping at every violent shout from the garden and every bottle that broke in the street.

I maybe could have stood one isolated night, the one occasional party. I'm sure I'd been to house parties that went on until the early hours when I was younger without giving much thought to the neighbours. But the next night my heart sank when, just as I was getting ready for bed, exhausted and cranky, the noise from next door started up again.

I soon realised the neighbour's daily pattern. He would wake up about midday, watch telly all afternoon, start loudly talking into his phone about 6 in the evening, get his mates round about 9 and then spend the rest of the night playing music, making a racket, laughing and shouting. If the noise stopped by 2am it was a good night. Weekends were worse, especially as the summer became hotter. Parties went on longer, party-goers were more numerous and more raucous. He would sit astride the wall in the back garden as if he owned it, fag hanging from his grinning lips, holding court in front of his band of jobless reprobates.

Over the next few weeks I tried everything. I complained to the letting agent in charge of the property. They said they would contact the owners. Some help they were! I leant my stereo speakers up against the wall and played Chas and Dave really loudly in the middle of the day to try and get my own back, or maybe to wake him up so he wouldn't be able to stay up so late. Pathetic, I know, but I was desperate. He didn't even stir. One night I waited for the noise to finish then poured a bottle of TCP through his letterbox in the dead of night, hoping to evict him by filling the house with its rancid smell. That afternoon I heard him throw the doormat into the front garden, joining the rest of the crap he'd dumped there, unperturbed, as if that happened at every place he lived.

Most nights I would end up covering my head with as many pillows as I could find, shouting into them: 'Shut up. Shut up! Just SHUT UP!'

By the time the papier-mâché head in my hands had taken form and started to look like that bastard from next door, I wanted to smash my fist right into his blank features. I painted it a sunburned red and inked that stupid tattoo up his neck, put three rings on his ears and drew on his smirking smile in a zig-zag shape with a marker pen. Finally, I found a couple of broken buttons and sewed them on for eyes. I placed the head on top of the torso, stepped back and looked at my creation.

It was him. I had made him and now he was mine.

Before I knew what I was doing I jumped on the effigy and pummelled his stuffed body, beating him with my fists, punching him again and again, spitting on him, screaming at him, kneeing him in the crotch until newspaper burst out of his seams. I was red-faced and dripping with sweat by the time I'd finished.

He sneered back at me, his broken button eyes staring coldly, vindictively.

'Fuck you!' I shouted and jabbed my finger right up the hole I'd made for his nose, gashing my hand on the ragged edge of the hardened paper, giving him a bloody nose. I retrieved my hand, shook away the pain and stormed out.

As I slammed the door behind me, just for a fraction of a second, I'm sure I heard him laugh.

***

We held the ran-tan on a Saturday when we knew more people would be around. It was the end of a hot summer's day and the air was heavy, close. I almost had second thoughts, wondering again if maybe we'd overreacted, but then their Friday night party kept me awake until 4 so I was overwrought with tiredness and anger and ready to kick up a fuss.

Word of the ran-tan got around because a group of 20, maybe 30, people gathered at the end of the street, hot and sticky in the oppressive heat, all enraged at the constant disturbance, or at not being able to open their windows in the summer sun because of the noise, or just angry on behalf of their neighbours. Most people had brought saucepans and wooden spoons to hit them with. Others had brought instruments. A middle-aged man had a trumpet by his side. An elderly woman held an old football rattle. A group of teenagers fidgeted impatiently with day-glo vuvuzela horns.

I dragged the effigy out by the neck and everyone commented approvingly on its similarity to the object of all our hatred. Someone called it the Ran-tan Man. I liked that.

We set fire to our torches, held the effigy aloft – its papier-mâché head lolling like a demented mannequin – and marched on number 63.

It was 9 in the evening and they were already in the throes of another party, shouting and thumping music emanating from the broken window. As we neared, one of us started banging their saucepan, then someone else, and, one by one, we all joined in.

We banged and stamped, rattled and clanged, we hollered and whooped.

The man with the trumpet played a loud and discordant flurry of random notes, his inflated face a bright crimson. The old woman twirled the rattle so hard she swayed with its weight, its clackety noise piercing the air. The vuvuzelas moaned and wailed in the hot summer night. It was a glorious cacophony, a symphony of pure vengeance.

Then the chanting started. It was the woman from over the road's ran-tan song and people soon caught on to her lyrics.

Ran-tan-tan
Sound of an old tin can
He bangs and bangs all night
So we'll set his house alight

We jabbed our hot flames into the air, faces flickering like demons.

If he does it any more
We'll bang down his front door
Holler, holler boys
If he makes another noise
We'll bang our pans around his head
And burn him til he's dead

My heart was beating loudly in my ears. I was giddy with the satisfaction of revenge. *That twat*, I thought, *deserves everything he gets*. I shouted the ran-tan song at the top of my voice letting the weeks of rancor roar from my exhausted body like fire.

The front door of number 63 slowly opened. His gormless face appeared from behind it, the lights of a dozen burning torches reflecting off his stupid bald head. He looked at the crowd of people staring angrily at him. He took in the banging and the clattering and the hooting directed at him. Then he looked up at the effigy of him being brandished by the mob.

He opened his mouth.

And he laughed.

His scrawny mouth laughed, making his three earrings twinkle in the red light.

He grinned his stupid grin, the swirly tribal tattoo on his neck twisting like a flame from his t-shirt, and closed the door again.

A wave of anger spread through the crowd. The noise from our pots and pans built to a crescendo. We shouted and shoved and surged toward the house like

a pack of wolves around their prey. Someone lit a banger and threw it at the door and the loud blast reverberated down the street. We trampled over his front garden and a couple of people pulled up the letting agent's sign and started hitting it against the door.

I grabbed the effigy to set light to it. I held it by the neck and put the flaming torch underneath its head but the material wouldn't catch. I looked at him, the Ran-tan Man, and he laughed at me with his charred inky grimace.

Then, faintly audible in the din of the crowd, a voice like spitting flames, I heard the Ran-tan Man hiss: 'Not meee! HIM-MMM!'

I dropped him to the floor, took a step back and looked at him. Then I looked at the broken window. My hands were shaking.

I knew what he wanted.

I threw the burning torch through the window and the tatty net curtains inside quickly flared up in a bright yellow blaze.

The crowd cheered.

Within minutes the bald man burst out of the door in a plume of black smoke, coughing and choking, closely followed by four of his mates. Without pausing, the man from across the road in the vest top emerged from the crowd and put his full weight behind a punch to the bald man's

stomach. He immediately bent double and fell to his knees. His mates got kicked and hit around their heads with saucepans until they legged it. The bald man gasped incredulously as his hands got tied to the pole of the uprooted 'To Let' sign and he was hoisted above the crowd like a pig on a spit roast.

I looked down at the Ran-tan Man, his limbs askew and head twisted up towards me. He growled at me again, sounding like a man with a pressed-down pillow on his face: 'Maaake him sssufferrr!'

I started chanting part of the ran-tan rhyme again – smashing the air with my fist, bellowing out the lyrics – and everyone joined in.

Holler, holler boys
If he makes another noise
We'll bang our pans around his head
And burn him til he's dead.

The bald man from next door was shouting and struggling as the crowd held him aloft. A wet stain appeared around his crotch and spread over his camo trousers.

The crowd jeered as one.

Without anyone leading, without anyone objecting, we carried him to the middle of the street and threw him to the ground where his face skidded along the hot tarmac.

We stood around him in a circle and laughed at him as he bled from his grazed nose. We shouted at him. Someone hit him on a leg with their pan, hard, leaving a dent in the metal.

I think maybe we could have left it there.

He would never have stepped foot in our street again, let alone in that house.

But the Ran-tan Man was still laughing at me. His limbs stuffed full of my hatred. His staring eyes broken pieces of revenge. My blood part of his. The scalded face became the bald man's, became mine.

'Finish meee!' he seethed.

I grabbed another torch and threw it at the tied-up bald man on the floor. It landed on his back and he kicked and screamed as his t-shirt caught fire.

The jeering died down and a grim silence took hold.

Someone else threw their burning torch at him, which lit up his terrified face. Then a storm of flames, a shower of wooden torches, rained down on him, thudded against him until a bright ball of writhing, screeching, spasming limbs flailed in front of us.

We watched him burn.

***

Now the effigy sits next to me on the sofa, his button eyes staring forward into the shaft of smoky daylight coming through the open window.

It's quiet next door but I haven't slept yet, he won't let me.

The acrid smell of burnt timbers and roasted flesh wafts through the room. The echoes from the man's screams last night still ring in my ears.

The Ran-tan Man's stuffed body slumps a little and his bulbous head turns and looks at me.

'Shut up,' I tell him.

The broken buttons burn a hole into my head.

'Shut up!' I shout at him.

The zig-zag pen mark across his face stretches into a smile.

'Just SHUT UP!'

THREAD

by Sinéad Persaud

Illustration by Claire L.Smith

T he notice was tattered *and barely stayed pinned up in the bitter London wind. Christmas advertisements and beseeching flyers for governesses cluttered every inch of bare space on the wooden post.*

It was no wonder why the humble, discoloured ad had been overlooked.

WANTED: DRESSMAKER'S APPRENTICE

I peered at the address on the notice, recognising the street name from some newspaper cutouts mum had kept in her journal. The site of one in a string of infamously-brutal Whitechapel murders that Scotland Yard had never been able to solve, even these fifteen years later. Sensationalised now through story, song and even theatre, many of my friends nev-er dared walk alone on the streets of Whitechapel even though the man colloquially dubbed 'The Ripper' hadn't struck in over a decade. Regardless, anyone with their wits about them would be cautious when traversing the unsavory streets of the East End.

I answered the notice. I'd become a talented seamstress over the years out of necessity.

When the weather was as cold as it was that early November day, my journeys tended to skew shorter. My legs, eager to escape the dagger-like beatings of the harsh wind, pushed themselves to their limits. I made my way the two miles from Bethnal Green to Whitechapel in under half an hour. Icicles of sweat clung to my brow by the time I arrived under the green awning of '**Ms. Orelia's Dress Shoppe**'.

I stopped outside the grimy window of the unremarkable facade. The window display housed a lined-up melange of fabric mannequins. All different heights and body types, wearing the most beautiful assortment of fashions made from the highest quality materials. Just the look of those rich silks and delicate laces rendered me giddy. The mannequins' faces were painted in extraordinary detail. And their eyes... something about their eyes struck me as uncanny.

Despite my unease, I pushed through the door, the trill of a bell alerting anyone inside to my presence.

And there I remained for months as Ms. Orelia's apprentice. Sewing on buttons and hemming fine dresses for the women who dared to travel to the little shop in this dingy dark corner of the East End. And oh, they would come. For Ms. Orelia was the best in all of London. A slight woman of indeterminable age with springs of dark unruly curls coming loose from her updo, she wore the sleeves of her blouse rolled up past her elbows revealing wisps of pale arms and surprisingly elegant hands. Those hands did the work of ten tailors in one day, and with me by her side to pick up the slack, she was unstoppable. Women and men and young girls with tears in their dresses and high society events to attend lamented the fact that Ms. Orelia closed up shop as soon as the sun began its descent.

'Won't you stay open a bit longer, please, I just have one more thing that needs mending!' they'd cry. But Ms. Orelia in her endearing but firm voice would deny their requests. Her rule was that we were to be out of the store by sundown. No exceptions. She would coil up the remainder of her special spool of thread and tuck it away into her drawer right as dusk began to fall. It was just one of the many idiosyncrasies that made Ms. Orelia such an enigmatic figure. I didn't give the rule much thought. After all, we were mere streets away from the site of one of the most gruesome of the Ripper murders. I simply took Ms. Orelia for a pragmatic woman who valued her safety and mine.

There was also the matter of the mannequins. Their haunting, looming presence in the shop had me constantly looking over my shoulder. I knew it was just the tawdry Penny Dreadfuls putting thoughts of the supernatural in my head, but oftentimes I would have sworn I saw them moving in the corner of my eye. And from my first day under the employ of Ms. Orelia, I felt a preternatural hum coming from somewhere within the shop. A buzzing sound that brought to mind summers with my cousins who'd long since moved away from London. Summers catching dragonflies that whirred and zipped by my head, sending the fine hairs of my ears into a tickled frenzy.

Despite the peculiar nature of my place of employment, I was happy for the first time since my mum had passed on. I'd finally be able to help in paying off some of my father's debts and maybe one day, I'd have saved enough to move somewhere far, far away. I could cope with a hum and an eccentric employer in exchange for a lick of hope.

***

February arrived, grey and desolate as usual. A winter morning in London right before dawn is not for the faint of heart. Though cloaked in a newly-darned wool coat (a Christmas gift from Ms. Orelia) and two pairs of socks, the spiteful cold soaked into my bones. Walking through the grey streets at this hour, one was privy to the aftermath of the strange sordid nights of the city. Glassy-eyed street sweepers numbly pushed their brooms down lanes filled with the trash of the previous night's exploits. Prostitutes tucked their most recent earnings away into pouches and hurried home to get a glimpse of their sleeping children before moving on to the next job. Drunks stumbled past them, their bottles nearing empty as their recollections of the night prior faded into oblivion.

I knocked on the shop's door to get Ms. Orelia's attention. So strict were her rules about not remaining after dark that she forbid me from having my own key. As I waited for her in the cold, I made sure to avert my eyes from the mannequins in the window, all attired in new fashions that served as Ms. Orelia's portfolio. I swore aloud once that their gazes followed me each morning as I passed by the window. Ms. Orelia simply tut-tutted at me and went on about how we young people think that everyone's eye is always upon us.

A hand on my shoulder elicited an unbecoming screech from my throat.

I turned to see a man, not much older than myself, stepping back with a look of shock on his face.

'I'm terribly sorry miss, I didn't mean to frighten you. I'm in a bit of a rush. Came by the shop last night but it was closed. I'll be requiring that lot of trousers I brought within the hour.'

I felt my cheeks go hot. My experience speaking with men was limited and I was terribly angry with myself that this particular interaction had begun with an outburst. Especially when his eyes were so kind and hazel and the slant of his smile so inviting.

Before I could say anything, Ms. Orelia brushed by me and clinked her key into the lock, bidding us both a curt good morning.

'Do come in,' I said. 'I apologise for my reaction. I was so very inside my own head for a moment.' I smiled, leading him inside.

'I understand entirely. Often I wonder which is actually real. This world or the one in my head. I'm in the theatre, you see, so things can get a bit ambiguous.' He winked.

I giggled, unable to come back with any clever repartee.

Ms. Orelia sent the young man on his way with six pairs of finely-hemmed britches fit for the players of Hamlet to don for their opening-night show that evening.

The rest of the day went on as usual. Fussy customers begging for a quick turnaround on a custom gown for a gala, a woman discreetly requiring her wedding dress be let out around the waist so as not to reveal her out-of-wedlock pregnancy. A young woman requesting jeweled embellishments on her stunning emerald-green evening gown. Since I was the same size as the client, I donned the gown so that Ms. Orelia could see exactly where she might add flourishes. For a moment I felt like a Queen.

During our afternoon tea, I tried another approach in an attempt to get Ms. Orelia to explain her sinister mannequins.

'The red haired woman who brought in her son's ripped breeches. She was at the market this past weekend. She mentioned how unsettling she found the mannequins in the window. Why not get rid of them if they are upsetting customers?' I asked between bites of my cucumber sandwich.

'I've tried,' Ms. Orelia said, sombrely. 'They just come back.'

Evening drew closer and so I began my end-of-day duties. Emptying the waste bin of scrap fabrics, tidying Ms. Orelia's sewing station and, finally, sweeping out front.

I hummed quietly as I collected the day's debris lying betwixt the cobblestones.

'Excuse me, miss?' A familiar voice sounded from behind me. I spun, clutching the broom tightly in my hand. It was the man from that morning. 'I didn't want to frighten you again so I made my best attempt to tread lightly!' He grinned impishly, tipping his hat.

'Was there something wrong with the garments? I'm afraid Ms. Orelia won't have time tonight to—'

'No, nothing of the sort. They were perfection. The director is very pleased,' he waved his arm as if to swipe away my concerns. 'I wondered if perhaps you might like to attend the play tomorrow evening? If you are concerned about the matter of a chaperone—'

'I'd love to!' I said before he could finish. Already a vision of the night was playing out in my mind at a breakneck speed. Velvet theatre curtains, daring swordplay, tearful monologues. A hand on the small of my back guiding me out of the playhouse, a chaste kiss on the cheek, the knowing averted gaze of a chaperone.

'Excellent. I shall see you here tomorrow evening then to escort you. Just about this time,' he tipped his hat again and strode past me. He turned back with a twinkle in his eye, 'My name is Simon, by the way. Pleasure to make your acquaintance.'

I gazed after him as he walked down the street, clad in his tattered but well-fitting navy blue coat. It took everything in me to wait until he was out of sight to let out a squeal of elation. Plucked out of obscurity by this strange but charming gentleman to attend a play! I must have been dreaming.

A rap on the glass broke me from my daydream. Ms. Orelia beckoned me inside.

'Quit dawdling, the sun is setting,' she said, shrugging into her burgundy coat. The seams were perfectly-tailored to her petite frame. Black velvet lapels tapering down the front into a line of thick brass buttons. For all my work helping to repair and tailor fine clothing in the shop, I still only owned two acceptable day dresses. I

watched the women who cycled through the shop in their high-quality fabrics and furs and dreamed of the day I'd be able to afford just a length of silk or a handful of silver buttons.

A terrible thought occurred to me. I had nothing to wear to the theatre. I'd sold all my mother's fine things and everything I owned had been restitched so many times it was a surprise that they didn't just fall off my body. There was nothing for it. When Simon came to call on me the following evening, I would have to refuse his invitation. I couldn't very well waltz into a theatre in my working clothes. My stomach sank and I pulled on my gloves and reached for my coat, dejectedly. As I tugged it on, a glimpse of emerald-green caught my eye. The evening gown.

It fit perfectly. And the customer wouldn't be back for it for another two weeks. Ms. Orelia wouldn't even notice it was missing as she had three other custom orders to work on by the week's end. All I needed to do was figure out a way to get it out of the store while she wasn't looking.

Or wasn't here at all.

The sun was rapidly disappearing behind the landscape of brick buildings. Ms. Orelia ushered me out the door like clockwork. She locked the shop door and bid me farewell, slipping the key into her handmade reticule purse.

'Get home safely,' she said without any warmth, but meaning the words all the same.

I had to think fast.

'Good night, Ms. Orelia!' I said, brightly. I made to walk past her, in the opposite direction of my home. I knocked into her, sending the purse flying from her hand. Making a show of tripping over my own feet, I fell atop the purse and fished out the key with a covert grace I didn't know I possessed.

When I stood, I handed her the drawstring purse.

'What am I thinking? East is west and

west is east to me today!' I giggled, dusting off my skirts and inspecting my gloves for tears. Unamused, Ms. Orelia sighed.

'Get some rest, I can't have you delirious in my shop.'

I dipped into an apologetic curtsey before walking off in the direction of home. Once I'd made it two-hundred metres from the storefront I slowed my pace, coming to a stop outside a pub on Dorset Street. The hustle and bustle of the early evening rendered me nearly invisible to passersby. Not dressed luridly enough to be tempting and not richly enough to be robbed, I blended into the grey scenery like a cobblestone.

I waited as the sun fell quickly, drenching the East End in ominous darkness. Though gas lights flickered on, the shadows they cast against the cheerless buildings felt menacing.

Creeping back onto the main street, I fished the key from my pocket and made my way to the shop. A mixture of exhilaration and terror swirled in my stomach as I heard the key click in the lock. The place was dreadfully haunting in the dim light and the mannequins loomed like churchyard statues in their window perch.

With haste I rushed to the tailoring rack and gently pulled the emerald-green dress from its hanger. The bodice was stiff in my hands, the boning made with remarkable care, while the silk skirts slithered like liquid. I held the fabric to my face and brushed it against my skin.

That's when I noticed the buzzing. I'd grown accustomed to the low hum that emanated from within the shop over the previous few months. But this was deafening, and only growing louder. I dropped the dress and covered my ears. I felt something grab at my hair and I spun to face my assailant.

The six mannequins stood in a semi-circle around me, their faces contorted into horrifying silent screams. I fell back-

wards, the heel of my boot tearing into the green skirt.

I scrambled to my feet, backing away from the army of fabric figures. Gathering the dress into my arms, I yelped as a rogue needle embedded in the fabric pricked my finger. I plucked the sharp point from my fingertip and let it go. It dangled from the strap of the emerald-green gown. I backed up further, maintaining as much distance from the mannequins as possible.

Was this some sort of trick Ms. Orelia was playing on me? A trap of some sort?

My breathing was ragged as my back touched the wall. I slid against it, trying to get around to the door. Though still as stone, the mannequin's lifelike eyes followed me as I slunk in the dark like a cornered animal.

I squeezed my eyes shut and made a beeline for the door. Just as my hand was about to close around the handle a searing pain shot through my abdomen. I looked down at my stomach in the dim light of the flickering street lamp outside the window. The needle I'd just wrenched from my finger shot through the thick wool of my coat. I reached down to try and catch it, but it turned back and pushed deeper into my flesh as though moved by an invisible hand.

I gasped in agony as I tried to pull it out, but to my horror the needle burrowed deeper. So deep that it was lost inside of me.

I shrieked, feeling the tiny sliver of metal twist wretchedly underneath my skin, as though turning itself around. It writhed about until it resurfaced, shooting through the fabric of my blouse.

I caught hold of the needle between my thumb and pointer finger—triumphant for merely a moment—before the needle, with some ungodly strength, forced its way into the tip of my finger. I screamed as it went through my bone as easily as a knife through a pat of butter. The thread zipped under my skin and in the dark I could see it. Revolting, like a maggot trying to burst free.

I tore at the thread, trying to separate it from the needle. I scrambled to Ms. Orelia's sewing table, shoving aside the mannequins and fumbled with the brass scissors as the needle made another stitch into my finger, making quick work of basting my entire hand. I cut at the thread, chopping again and again. But the thread remained steely, weaving its way up my left arm. I could barely see it, it laced through me so fast. I watched as my hand dulled in colour, the texture becoming rough as cotton. With a sinking, out of body feeling, I witnessed the skin of my hand turn into fabric.

The needle shot through my neck and I fell to the ground, paralysed.

I lay in agonising torture as the needle stitched up my entire body. All I could do was silently sob, a puddle forming right underneath my cheek that lay pressed into the cold ground. The wraithlike needle finally reached my face. I prayed, as the needle sewed my lips shut, that soon I would find peace. That death would take me; another nameless victim of Whitechapel.

But that didn't happen.

I lay on the ground all night. Unable to move anything except for my eyes, which darted back and forth, hoping someone might see me through the window and take pity. The mannequins hovered above me in a ritualistic circle. My vision was blurry, fading in and out.

I thought of Ms. Orelia, finding me the next day. Surely this was the end of my employment with her. She'd see that I'd stolen her key and I'd be sent away without my week's wages, if not charged for criminal activity.

Morning crept around again and I heard the bell on the door signal an arrival. Relieved and terrified, I waited for Ms. Orelia to help me up and hopefully take me to the surgeon's.

'Not again,' I heard her say, quietly. She hoisted me up from the ground with shocking ease.

Why couldn't I move? Why couldn't I...

My eyes fell on the long mirror propped up against the east wall. The one that customers used to ogle themselves in Ms. Orelia's finished handiwork. I was nowhere to be found in the reflection.

Instead there was a new mannequin. My skin had turned to an olive-toned fabric the consistency of burlap, and my eyes were glassy and surreal. I felt tears well, but there was nowhere for them to go. I wasn't real anymore.

Ms. Orelia put me in the window display that same day, dressed in a smart, billowing winter coat and feathered hat.

I watched her reflection in the glass window as she scooped up the torn green dress and mended it skillfully. I listened as customers filed into the shop and commented on the brand-new mannequin in the display.

The work day wound down and daylight waned. A familiar figure strode up the cobblestone street and stopped outside the shop. For a moment, Simon and I locked eyes. He cocked his head and furrowed his brow before entering the shop.

'She isn't here anymore,' Ms. Orelia told him, with no hint of a lie.

'That new figure in your window. It looks remarkably like—'

'I know. I made it in her likeness. I like to keep all of my assistants with me in that way. They are, after all, like my children!' She smiled at him briefly before brushing past him to start the closing duties.

Simon left. He gave one last glance back at me in the window before shaking his head and disappearing into the foggy night.

I screamed and screamed after him, but the only sound that came out was a barely-discernible hum.

CONTRIBUTORS

★ ★ ★

MIKE ADAMSON holds a doctoral degree from Flinders University of South Australia. After early aspirations in art and writing, Mike returned to study and secured qualifications in marine biology and archaeology. Mike has been a university educator since 2006, is a passionate photographer, master-level hobbyist and journalist for international magazines.

TIMOTHY GRANVILLE was born in the New Forest, England, and now lives in rural Wiltshire, where he enjoys inflicting prehistoric sites on his wife and daughter. His most recent stories have appeared in *Crooked Houses* (Egaeus Press), *Oculus Sinister* (Chthonic Matter) and *Dark Lane Anthology 10*. His short story 'The Path Through the Woods' appeared in *The Ghastling's* Book Eleven.

VERITY HOLLOWAY is a speculative fiction and historical non-fiction author based in East Anglia, England. She has two novels to her name – *Pseudotooth* and *Beauty Secrets of The Martyrs* – and a non-fiction book *The Mighty Healer*: a biography of her Victorian quack doctor cousin. Verity's short stories have been published in publications including *Animal Literary Magazine, Far Horizons* and *The Ghastling,* and she currently writes folklore features for *Hellebore* Zine. Her short story 'Florabelle' appeared in *The Ghastling's* Book Ten.

JANICE LEADINGHAM grew up in the Smoky Mountains of Tennessee, USA, and majored in feminism and fairy tales in college. You can find her listening to Dolly Parton, watching horror films or writing and researching death folklore. Right now, she is probably reading Shirley Jackson. She currently lives in Portland, Oregon, with her exceptionally-kind husband and their two special-needs pets. A descendant of three of the accused Salem witches, when asked what she wanted to be when she grew up, she said 'a witch.'

ANNA OJINNAKA is a lab assistant who has fancies of one day becoming a scream queen.

SIMON JOHN PARKIN is a graphic designer by trade, living in Somerset, England, with his partner and son. He grew up in the English Midlands and also spent ten years in Brighton, where his hatred of noisy neighbours began. He is previously unpublished but has always written weird stories and made little books, zines and films.

SINÉAD PERSAUD is an Indian-American actor, writer and proud Ouija Board owner from Boston, Massachusetts, USA. While studying film and television production at NYU's Tisch School of the Arts, Sinead interned at *SNL, The Colbert Report* and multiple film festivals. Post-NYU, Sinéad moved to Los Angeles to participate in the NBC Page Program and soon after co-founded the popular literary/historical comedy YouTube channel *Shipwrecked Comedy.* Sinead co-wrote and starred in the series *Edgar Allan Poe's Murder Mystery Dinner Party*, which received praise from *AV Club, Nerdist,* and *Tor. com.* Sinéad is a Sundance New Voices Lab alum and has recently had a horror story produced on the *No Sleep Podcast.*

MATTHEW G. REES is the author of the story collections *Keyhole* and *Smoke House & Other Stories.* His plays *Dragonfly* and *Sand Dancer* have been performed professionally. In a varied life, Rees has – among other things – been a journalist and a teacher. He lived and worked in Moscow, Russia, for a period, prior to a PhD at the University of Swansea, Wales, where he explored the influence of mentally-held imagery on the writing of short fiction. He currently lives in Wales. More at *www.matthewgrees.com*

ASHLEY STOKES is a writer based in the east of England. He is the author of *Gigantic* (Unsung Stories, 2021), *The Syllabus of Errors* (Unthank Books, 2013) and *Voice* (TLC Press, 2019), and editor the *Unthology* series and *The End: Fifteen Endings to Fifteen Paintings* (Unthank Books, 2016). His recent short fiction includes 'Subtemple' in *Black Static;* 'Hardrada' in *Tales from the Shadow Booth*, Vol 4 edited by Dan Coxon; 'Evergreen' in *BFS Horizons 11;* 'Yellow Haze' in *Strands Literary Hub,* 'Two Drifters' in *Unsung Stories Online,* and 'Black Lab' in *Storgy.* His stories have also appeared in *Bare Fiction, The Lonely Crowd, The Warwick Review* and more. He has short fiction forthcoming in *Black Static, Nightscript, Out of Darkness* (edited by Dan Coxon, Unsung Stories), and *Ceci nest pas une Histoire D'Horreur* (edited by JD Keown, Night Terror).

ZUZANNA KWIECIEN is an illustrator and designer. With her practice, she aims to develop bodies of work that capture the visual narrative of the subject and combine it with a distinct atmosphere. As an artist, she values time and effort put into the construction of a high-quality work of art. Find her on Instagram at @ firstaidkiddo. *www.behance.net/zuzannakwiecien*

CLAIRE L. SMITH is an Australian author, visual artist and designer. Her artwork draws from themes of the occult, the macabre and the morbidly beautiful while appearing in works from *The Ghastling Press, Tenebrous Press, Off Limits Press, Haley Newlin* and more. Her debut gothic horror novella, *Helena* was released from CLASH Books in 2020 with her next horror novella coming from Off Limits Press in October 2021. *www.clairelsmith.com*

ANDREW ROBINSON is a printmaker and graphic designer. A self-taught artist specialising in linocut prints, his interests and influences stem from wildlife, mythology, and all things creepy or otherworldly. Andrew hails from the east coast of Canada and now lives in Oxford, England, with his partner and daughters. A selection of his work can be seen at monografik. ca and on Instagram *@eaglesnakefight.*

REBECCA PARFITT has worked in publishing for over a decade. Her debut poetry collection, *The Days After*, was published by Listen Softly London in 2017. She is currently working on a book of macabre short stories for which she won a Writers' Bursary from Literature Wales in 2020. Two stories from this collection were published in *The New Gothic Review* in 2020. Her first film, *Feeding Grief to Animals*, was commissioned in 2020 by the BBC & Ffilm-CymruWales. She lives in the Llynfi Valley, Wales, with her partner and daughter. *rebeccaparfitt.com*

RHYS OWAIN WILLIAMS is a writer and editor from Swansea, Wales. His first poetry collection, *That Lone Ship*, was published by Parthian in 2018. Rhys also runs *The Crunch* – a multimedia poetry magazine (*crunchpoetry. com*). In addition to all things ghastly, Rhys is interested in folklore, urban myth and psychogeography. He lives in a terraced house near the sea with his partner and a black cat named Poe. *rhysowainwilliams.com*

WALLACE MCBRIDE is a graphic designer from South Carolina, USA. His work has been featured in *Fangoria*, The Sleepy Hollow International Film Festival, The Boston Comedy Festival, the Associated Press, the U.S. Army and dozens of newspapers in the United States, and also used on official merchandise for *The Prisoner* and *Star Trek*. He is the creator of The Collinsport Historical Society, a website dedicated to the cult television series *Dark Shadows*. Since its launch in 2012, The Collinsport Historical Society has been recognised numerous times by The Rondo Hatton Classic Horror Awards, and received The Silver Bolo Award in 2020 from Shudder's *The Last Drive-In with Joe Bob Briggs*. Wallace sometimes uses the handle 'Unlovely Frankenstein', which is either a pseudonym or just the name of his Etsy store. He isn't sure yet. *www.unlovelyfrankenstein.com*

APRIL-JANE ROWAN is an author, editing assistant for Gurt Dog Press and social media co-ordinator for both Gurt Dog Press and *The Ghastling*. She was born with a morbid fascination that she turned into writing so she could explain away her strangeness. Luckily for her, she found she rather liked it, so for many years she has been creating bizarre, dark tales. Her books *Beneath A Bethel* and *Lovelorn* are available from Gurt Dog Press. When not writing, she can be found lurking in graveyards, libraries and museums. She lives in Sweden with her two partners and their pack of beasties. Follow her on Instagram at *@theliterarychamber*

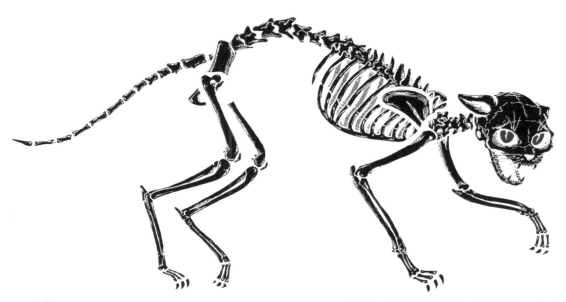

It's Amazing!

The low cost of supporting

The Ghastling!

For just pennies a day you can support
the morbid interests of horror fans all over the world

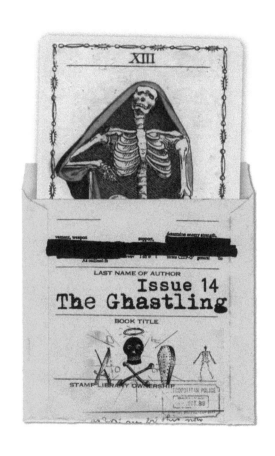